The Big Book of Post-Collapse Fun

Rachel Sharp

Editor

Fallon Clark

Cover Art

Jessi Sheron

Additional Copy Editing

Barnaby Felton, Brandon Sharp

ISBN: 151520247X
ISBN-13: 978-1515202479

DEDICATION

To the Clandestine Circus
You know who you are

CONTENTS

PROLOGUE
FRAGS OF A PAST LIFE

I'll tell you the truth: I wish it had been zombies.

The zombie apocalypse always looks like so much fun in the movies. The heroes (who naturally include a nursing student, a redneck hunter, an electrician, a biologist, and an ex-military strategist who just happened by) band together and start shooting. There's all the canned food they can eat and all the hospitals full of medical supplies they might want. The biologist falls in love with the nursing student after saving her from a deadly zombie bite. Everyone goes home happy.

What happened here wasn't the zombie apocalypse, but let me say something about those hospitals full of supplies: when there's a real emergency, they *use* that shit.

Once the zombie apocalypse strikes, there are no bodies. There's just living good guys and dead bad guys. Almost like nothing terrible really happened. I can't think of any other disaster with that perk. Mostly, people are just dead. Sometimes they hang out and rot for a while. Sometimes you find them burnt to a crisp and still holding a perfectly unscathed beer bottle in their crispy fingers.

But I'm getting ahead of myself.

Before I hand over my idiot adventures, I wanted to give some kind of blurry snapshot of Life Before the Suck.

Picture a twenty-something redhead. Recent college graduate. Unemployed. Living in a third-floor apartment in Portland, Oregon. There's a porch attached to the apartment by a couple of slanted two-by-fours and held together by fifty years of cheap paint, and she's sitting on it with her friends. One is in the process of dying her hair blue and looks like a smurf starlet. One is trying to talk herself off of Pinterest and into finishing a ten-page paper. One is chain-smoking and nodding while the redhead tells her about the dangers of carcinogenic make-up.

They've all got cups of healthy, invigorating tea beside them, going stone cold while they drink corner-store box wine instead. They're using plastic champagne glasses because everything else is dirty. Somewhere under the pile in the sink there are real cups, sticky with homemade smoothie residue, but the mountain of dishes has been there so long that the leaves falling from multitudinous houseplants have started to camouflage it. Recycled plastic-ware and compostable paper cups are on the counter. An ivy plant is very slowly trying to eat them.

The owner of this kitchen has a completely reasonable explanation about how it is not, in fact, dirty. It's organic, earthy, and self-regulating. Natural . . . Zen . . . Something about decentralized compost. It makes sense at the time.

The kitchen echoes laughter from the porch.

The ladies outside are cracking up so hard that wine is sloshing onto the floorboards. They're pointing and waving at a man in boxers wandering down the street and playing a guitar. This is the real laughter—Girl's club laughter—shared only with female friends and the kind of significant other you're willing to pee in front of. It's loud, full of snorts and idiot giggling fits, raucous laughter second only to that of hyenas. Eyes start to tear up. Tea is knocked over. Hands are thrown up in surrender and cigarettes are stubbed out in submission. The wandering boxer minstrel launches into "Blister in the Sun" and turns south at the end of the block.

The end-of-summer gathering ends. Three of these girls go back to college in Seattle. One stays home.

Poor little Mab, all by herself.

It's not quite fair to say I was alone after that. I took classes and made the kind of friends you never exchange phone numbers with. I went out with a fuckhead or two from online dating sites. I finally learned the name of at least one bartender at the Triple Nickel (home of the giant Jenga game that scares the patrons every time someone loses). I dated another fuckhead who seemed amazing until he tried to move in uninvited and ate all my food. It's much easier to notice a potential mate's flaws when they're devouring the last of the cheesecake. I was saving that cheesecake for a special occasion. Like a Tuesday.

When I booted him out, he stole all my condoms.

I joined several online feminist groups, but each time a local meeting came around I found myself suddenly motivated to do things like mop the sticky kitchen or write an unscheduled blog entry. I believe in treating women like human beings, but the bottom line is that I don't really like human beings all that much, especially in groups larger than three, so I treated my new politically-active acquaintances accordingly by staying home and avoiding all contact. To behave any other way towards them would have demonstrated a strong gender bias.

I tried to befriend a girl I saw at the bar a lot, despite

the fact that her vocabulary seemed to consist of "Um," "Eh," "Yeah," "Maybe," and "Right on, sister." Hours into a night of drinking, I told her that I had decided to start referring to my most recent boyfriend as 'fuckhead #1,' not because he was chronologically first but because he was clearly primary among them, the king of the fuckheads. She got confused and settled for "Right on, sister." I warmed to the idea of looking for a new bar.

There's got to be one for me somewhere. One where they play Amanda Palmer and Elvis Costello, and know that an egress is not a bird. Where I can use the word 'hypothetically' with abandon.

Well, there probably isn't one anymore. I'm sad that I never found that bar.

But I was talking about Life Before the Suck.

A lot of my time was spent job-hunting, a method of torture in which a person runs around town handing out paper copies of her life, which are then promptly shredded, thrown out, or possibly recycled into something more useful. Occasionally, someone will read this piece of paper and contact her so that they can judge and dismiss her in person. The idea is that one of these people will fail to dismiss her, and instead employ her. This almost never happens. When it does, she will then spend a large percentage of her waking life doing menial tasks in exchange for 'money,' which can take paper form but more often exists only in the aether. Money can be exchanged for goods. Three hours of labor can be exchanged for a pizza. Ten hours of work can be exchanged for a chair. It would have been faster to cut down a tree and make the damn chair oneself, but that's how things were done.

Job-hunting could be improved somewhat by going to school for things like auto repair, bartending, or hairdressing, which of course I did not do. I went to college and majored in Philosophy. Philosophy is not something you really *do.* Ideally, those who can't do, teach. Those who can't teach, waitress. Unfortunately, in the years before the Suck, pretty much everyone who wasn't a mechanic, bartender, or hair stylist was stuck trying to waitress. Dog-walking, gas station attending, dish washing, and floor cleaning were also acceptable things to 'do' while your soul grew moldy around the edges and the expensive education slowly turned to sedimentary sludge between your ears.

But I didn't have any of these things to 'do.' So I racked up credit card debt spending money I didn't have and procrastinated the Great American Novel and fiddled with my feminist gaming blog instead.

Most mornings I'd get a breakfast sandwich and a newspaper. I couldn't really afford it, but somehow going out made me feel like I still had a life, and doing the crossword made me feel like I still had a brain.

In one of those newspapers, there was an article about the geological state of the planet. I skimmed it. Seismologists were talking about potential increases in instability under the United States. For some reason, the paper had also interviewed meteorologists about climate change. What was the point? I just wanted to feel superior for knowing that forty-nine across was Cormorant. I turned the page.

Of course, it's easy now to say that I should have read the damn article. And pretend I would have done something. Like I would have read a sixty-word blurb, realized what was going to happen, and done something smart about it.

It's so easy to get sidetracked.

Let me leave it at this.

Picture poor little Mab, all alone, on that same porch. The crossword is finished beside her, and it's Sunday so she's feeling pretty accomplished. Being unemployed, it seems like an accomplishment just to know what day it is.

There's tea again, double-spice chai, and this time she's actually drinking it. It's raining. The porch is covered, but she's pulled her feet under her in the splintering wooden thrift-store chair to avoid splashing water coming off the roof. She's waiting for a message from someone on OKCupid, who will probably turn out to be Fuckhead #48 but for now is just a cute boy on the other side of the internet. There is possibility. The kitchen has been cleaned because her inner house wife is on the upswing and beating her inner hippie with a broom. She feels like a responsible adult. One with yet another day off. There is tea. There are cookies. There are pajama pants and piano music and the rain is not too cold.

This happened. It happened to me. It was real.

And it may not help me to remember that, but damned if I'm going to let it go.

CHAPTER ONE
NATURAL DISASTERS: A RECAP

Let me fucking tell you: I was not ready.

It's a funny thing, living in America. A girl gets to thinking that it's the whole world. Other countries aren't really countries. They're vacation destinations, or political news. America was the only real place, because I was in it.

Now I have to think "America" the same way that I think "Pangaea." The United States are no longer united. Well, let's face it, Hawaii and Alaska might as well have been alien planets in the first place, but the rest of it . . . we were all in it together. Texas might not be like home, but you could drive there. New York Republicans, homophobic rednecks, Hollywood starlets- these people were practically my brothers and sisters compared to a stranger living in Iceland. There might be someone in Russia who would have been a soul mate, a twin, an idol, but that person wasn't really real. At best, anyone who lived in a place I couldn't drive to was hypothetical.

Once the apocalypse started, as far as I knew, anyone north of Mount Saint Helens or south of Powell Boulevard was hypothetical.

The pieces I divide the world up into are now much

smaller. The barriers are all new. For one thing, a large bit of F. Scott Fitzgerald's beloved Midwest fell into the great American water reservoir. It just sunk. Like it tried to pee at 2 a.m. but someone left the toilet seat up.

That was the last news I got before sources of information went from major media to survivor scraps. There were still some idiots out there wasting their batteries taking cell phone photos and uploading them to what was left of the internet. My connection to the Great and Powerful Internet Tubes was dead in the wall, but during the Suck my phone still worked and some sites were still up.

Hodgepodge evidence seemed to suggest that the New Madrid Fault Line (which I didn't even know we had) was now more of a trench. There was a huge ongoing disaster between myself and the Eastern Seaboard.

I was never going to see New York again.

For some reason, that thought wasn't the strange one. So I'd never see New York again. So what? Might have happened that way anyway. Know what the weird thought was?

I no longer lived in the Northwest. The frame of reference that told me I did was now a whole new shape, not even a thing. Atlantic City might as well be Atlantis, for all it mattered. There is nothing to be northwest *of* anymore. The only thing I could say was that I probably live in the North. There must still be an equator. Of course, if the magnetic poles switched or something, I'm wrong again and I now live in the Deep South.

The things I knew were as follows: Something bad was happening. My name was Mab. I lived on Northeast Prescott Street, Portland, Oregon, 97211, and as of yet, I had not gone anywhere.

Now where the hell was I?

I would love to be able to transcribe for you a play-by-play of the total reshaping of Earth as I knew it (an event which I have come to consistently refer to in my head as The Suck). When it started, there were news stories, graphs, and public service announcements. The internet fell all over itself with memes and animated .gifs, photoshopping kittens into every new stunning disaster picture.

As far as I can tell, the chronological order of events was something like this:

A news story cropped up about the San Andreas Fault doing things it wasn't supposed to. Some small chunk of California was shifting ponderously on the wrong axis. It was barely measurable, but we're talking about geology here. The California coastline drifting north at two inches a year had previously been a fascinating bit of trivia. When several minor earthquakes chased each other's tails up and down the coast, reporters went straight to geologists and geologists said, "It's weird! It's weird and that's important! We're still figuring out why." This was dutifully reported. Residents in affected areas mocked the rest of the country for making a big deal out of a minor shakedown or two. There was some discussion of broadening the areas where earthquake-proof buildings should be considered, followed by political arguments about infrastructure and spending. Mostly I just remember a lot of angry governors, yelling at each other through cameras. The second half of the front page covered geology junk every few days for a while, which, as it related to me personally, was first used as a coaster for my vanilla chai and later became the drop cloth for re-potting my plants.

Yes, I curse myself. I was just in it for the crossword

puzzles. Sometimes the Sudoku, if I wanted to make myself feel really stupid. Everyone should have been paying attention, but I didn't because I never thought it would be relevant to me. I was more interested in news about legislation concerning workplace gender discrimination. Each new battle in the GOP's War on Women seemed earth-shattering. If I'd known the earth was actually shattering, I would have looked into that, too.

Geologists across the world started reporting a plethora of anomalous readings. Second-page news. Nobody cared, until an anomalous lake temperature reading became a brand new volcano. In Memphis.

I remember that one better than anything before, or anything that followed. Suddenly pictures of fit people on bikes and charming craft fair booths disappeared from the front page of my precious paper. Stories about red ink in the state ledger were replaced by gratuitous use of the real thing. There was a photograph labeled Zodiac Park. The color of the sky seemed wrong in a way I could feel in my gut, even through a photograph. Under that sky, there was a volcano. It looked so small. Apparently, they do, when they're first starting out: Volcanoes grow like living things. I guess disaster movies and crazy digital manipulation jobs had skewed my perspective. It seemed like if it wasn't a few hundred feet high, it couldn't really be dangerous, but it must have been. Buildings were on fire. Cars were wrecked. In the foreground of the photo, a man was running, carrying a small child and a large bag. Somewhere in the middle ground, out of focus, was a dirty white smudge that my imagination swears to this day was a dead Elvis impersonator, lungs full of ash, never to croon again.

I ducked back inside and went straight to my desk to open a browser window, traditionally my best research tool. What I got wasn't entirely accurate, or even plausible, but I knew how to dig until the internet told me everything I needed to know. There were more photos: Cars on 40 trying to get across the bridge. The Shelby County Forensic Medical building taking a lava bomb to the face. Most people had evacuated in time. When talking about geological events, 'instantaneous' can also mean 'over the course of a few days.' It should also be noted that while a lot of people will resist evacuation when it comes to hurricanes and similar (because they just *know* that it won't be as bad as the news anchor says, *that pussy*), watching lava roll down the tarmac at the airport does tend to focus the mind on grabbing the cat, the laptop, and the vinyl collection before running like hell. There was a photo of a traffic jam on the highway. Many people had strapped furniture to their cars. I don't know where they thought they were going to put it down again.

The population of the New Madrid Fault parted like a drag queen's wig. I can't say for sure what happened to them after that. I know that in the following weeks, Michigan became a chain of islands in one big Great Lake, so anyone who took this chance to impose on their relatives in Kalamazoo probably didn't fare too well. Last I knew, the Carolinas were still a thing, so some of them may have lucked out. Anyone who made it to New York might still be there, unless they were stupid enough to take up beachfront property in a time of seismic upheaval. The last graphic I saw on the news, though, seemed to suggest that the entire Eastern Seaboard may now lean slightly to the west.

It occurs to me that my old apartment in Brooklyn, which was tilted to begin with, is now either leaning enough to make a resident grow one leg longer than the other, or has been corrected and is now the only level building in New York.

My current apartment was fine at this point. Everyone seemed to have fled the neighborhood while I was sleeping, and the other side of the street suffered some kind of electrical fire, but otherwise my block was intact. It didn't even flood. When the dust clouds and thunderstorms came through, one just washed away the other and everything ran south, on its way to do some kind of damage that made scary noises but was otherwise imperceptible from this far up. I'd heard a transformer blow once when I was a kid, and chalked up most of the bigger, more frightening booms to that. There was another one snapping and buzzing down the street, waiting to explode. I wanted to climb on the roof to get a better look, but the roof is scary at the best of times. In an ongoing storm, with no one else around to call 911 if my stupid ass fell off the ladder, the idea of going up on the roof made my stomach turn to lead. I didn't even go to the edge of the porch anymore. I never realized how comforting it was to know that someone would call 911 for me if the need arose. Knowing that there is no 911 anymore makes lighting a god damn candle feel like skydiving with a homemade parachute. I remember feeling like this the first time my health insurance ran out. Everything is dangerous. I'd been wearing my slip-resistant house shoes since the power went out. The kitchen floor seemed too hazardous to cross without them.

Some of the people must have run west when the New Madrid Fault started to buck them off, and for those bastards I feel sorriest of all. They just knew that they'd made it to safety. At least, they knew it for a day or two. Then they found out that they'd scrabbled out of the frying pan and into the total clusterfuck. The middle of the

United States dropped between ten and two-hundred feet. Most structures and even forests fought gravity as they were thrown up and shoulder-checked over, crushing each other like the world's slowest dominos. The rest of Americans felt another collective earthquake and looked around, asking each other, "What now?" The combination dust clouds and thunderstorms spread out in all directions. If seen from the sky and sped up, it would have looked like the largest mushroom cloud in the history of mankind. And we've made a few.

There was still some kind of media for a while after that, and stories emerged of heroic men rescuing families in single-engine planes that somehow took off from tilted little hick airfields. Women who commandeered river boats and made it all the way to Baton Rouge. Apparently some people drove more than a thousand head of cattle into Texas right before most of Oklahoma sunk, taking with them what were probably the only horses to make it out of the middle states alive.

The rest of the population were mostly crushed by their own houses.

Here's a quick run-down of the things you do while trapped in your apartment because the world is going to hell:

Take stock of all the food you have. Calculate how long it could last you. Think about eating all the perishable stuff first while you absent-mindedly eat your last can of peach halves. Realize what you're doing. Yell "Fuck!" loudly. Stand stunned in your kitchen, realizing that you don't know what you're supposed to do. Stand around with the fridge door open, counting your leftovers, until you realize that the power's out and you're letting all the cold out of the magical cold-making box. Yell some more.

Decide to put a piece of duct tape on the fridge door to remind yourself not to open it. Discover that you don't have any duct tape. Find some knitting yarn on the kitchen table and have the brilliant idea to tie that around the fridge instead. Try to move the fridge away from the wall in order to get the rope around it. Let out a scream that sounds like a cross between three ducks and an eighties pop star when you tip over the fridge, spilling your food all over the kitchen. Crawl under the table like you did when you were little. Cry. Not in a classy single-teardrop way. Cry like it's the first day of your period and you just got in a fight with your best friend. Try to stuff the leftover ziti back into its Tupperware. Get the fridge upright despite the crippling fear that you're going to crush yourself. Clean up your mess. Stare at your kitchen. Wander off.

Remember that you're supposed to fill the bathtub with clean water in case you don't get any more. Do this. Get worried about 'stuff' getting into the water. Cover the bathtub in saran wrap. Realize you probably should have taken one last hot shower first, approximately one second before it occurs to you that the hot water is already gone and soon you'll be screwed for cold water, too. Cry again because you already miss hot showers.

Sit down on your bed with a notepad to make a list of Things to Do. Stare at blank paper. Fall asleep instead.

Wake up. See that it's dark out. Try to turn on your beside lamp. Repeat. Use the light from your cell phone to find a candle. Worry about your cell phone battery. Light a candle that's labeled "Invigoration" but smells like burning cat hair. Light five more candles and spread them all over the apartment. Change your mind, bring them all into the kitchen. Loiter in the kitchen. Realize that earlier, you screamed several times and nobody knocked or called the cops.

Panic. Try to call someone. Listen to the buzzing, useless white noise your brain makes while it tries to puzzle out the "Emergency Calls Only" message on your phone. Dial 911. Forgo listening to your brain's feedback loop in favor of the curious noises your phone makes . . . Ring, click. Ring, click. Ring, click. Hang yourself.

Up. I mean hang up. Not hang yourself.

Look outside. Notice the lack of cars on the street. Wonder if there was some kind of official evacuation notice that you missed while you were perusing disaster photos online or if all your neighbors just removed themselves on their own initiative.

Go out on the porch, intending to yell until someone finds you. Have an internal debate about the odds of being found by a serial killer. Decide to yell anyway.

Find that the sheer embarrassment instilled in you by a lifetime of having to be civilized and cool has taken away your childhood ability to yell in public when all that comes out of you is "Hello?" It goes out into the world at approximately the same decibel level as the proverbial cat's meow.

Punch 911 into your phone one more time.

Dial. Ring. Click. Ring. Click.

West-coast news sources went down first. East-coast news sources covered the story that west-coast news services had gone down. Soon after that, they dwindled to automated messages and hardcore journalists who were gradually going crazy trying to figure out the odds of dying at their post. The Great and Powerful Internet started to go down, handfuls of servers at a time. The following is some of the news that I received in the week or two following The Suck. I can't vouch for any of it. At least P.S. (Pre-Suck) I could believe that the worst of the bullshit was called out by a competing news source.

At any rate, here are things that may be true:

The President of the United States was alive in a bunker somewhere at the beginning of the New Madrid Fault event. He recorded several speeches, each one so predicable that he may have taken them straight from the disaster movie screenplay that his speech-writer was undoubtedly working on since his or her days as an English teacher. At least one of these speeches was badly corrupted before it could be broadcast, and the attempt at digital reconstruction resulted in a three-minute chunk of Addressing the Nation that was so pixelated I thought I was watching someone play Minecraft.

The last article posted on Jezebel, a signing-off entry in what was starting to look like an extinction-level event, was a brilliant if somewhat hysterical piece called "Earth is a Mother," which included some news from the rest of the world. Parts of Canada were having just as many problems as we were, seeing as major geological shifts tend to give not a single fuck about arbitrarily assigned borders. Japan had made some progress toward solving the housing crisis by getting taller and broader almost overnight, popping up out of the ocean like an erection at a hot tub party. All of this sounds like good news for Hello Kitty and thousands of identically-dressed businessmen until you consider the volcanoes. Of course, the tidal wave from this side of the ocean may have helped them put down some fires. Australia was doing all right so far, but staring down the barrel of a loaded hurricane. Most of Great Britain was evacuating to the Continent, which must have seemed like a great idea before news of the impending crunch into Russia broke. Some place called Kotelny Island imploded. And we should be looking forward to the impact of all this hitting Antarctica, which may then proceed to knock itself to ice cubes and make a nice big tidal wave for all of us in the process.

I've seen a lot of CG natural disasters in my life, so I think I managed to pick most of the fake screenshots from the real photos. Still hardly counts as the sort of valuable and reliable information I'd want to pass on, though, so for now I think I'll refrain from speculation. Towards the end, I was starting to call bullshit on photos that I'm now convinced were one-hundred-percent legitimate. If you've ever seen a disaster movie where an adult toy store gets washed into a church down the street, please let me know, but the odds are against it. I'm pretty sure if I'd ever seen a dildo in a collection plate floating down the block, I'd remember.

By the time the internet really started to fall apart, some cowardly bit of me was ready to see it happen. My phone had started to give off a sinister vibe. I'd give it a sidelong look as it blinked on my kitchen table and think of the evil computers and robots that once dominated science fiction. I wondered what it was thinking. I could almost hear it talking each time the battery light flashed. *Die. Die. Die.* Asimov's laws, gone the way of 911 and the buffalo.

Last I knew, people were fleeing one state only to get swallowed by the earth in another one. Everyone started talking at cross-purposes about the safest place to be. The government said stay home. Enough people were dead by then that everyone seemed to think the worst was over because, well, it had to be . . . how much worse could it get? The National Guard and assorted rescue operations did their thing until there weren't enough left to save each other when an area went bad and the people in it went tharn.

Even after my last news input stopped putting out, I was never quite sure what had happened. I was left holding a fistful of barely-educated guesses in my dark, creaking apartment. And now I'm passing those tattered scraps of informational currency on.

What I could vouch for at that point was Portland, Oregon, east of the Willamette. I can say that I took my screwy little moped down to the Fremont Bridge and it was decidedly unstable. I couldn't see any of the other bridges. I knew there were other ways to cross a river, but I always drown when I try it in video games and I found that sufficiently discouraging.

I tried to go north. Once I found the bridge to Washington intact, something possessed me and I tried to just take my little moped on a great journey, all the way to Alaska if I could, riding off into what looked like the sunset but clearly wasn't.

The red glow turned out to be Mount Saint Helens. She's talking out of the other side of her face these days, and it looks like she vaporized Silver Lake before bringing it all the way to I-5 and moving her magma in for good. What a bitch.

Headed south. Powell Boulevard now seemed to be a branch of the Willamette River that continuously overflowed its south bank. Once again, Oregon Trail taught me never to mess with that. I went home.

With the moped parked beside the house, I finally got up the nerve to knock on my neighbor's doors. Apartments 1A and 1B, no answer. The door to 2B wasn't even closed. The crazy world I was living in started to feel less like a spontaneous evacuation and more like a Rapture.

My apartment seemed like the best place to be. I ran back and hid in my room.

Opened the shades to let light in.

Closed them to shut the world out.

Opened them again when I started picturing all the horrible things that I wouldn't be able to see coming with the shades closed.

After several repetitions of this, I started to roll my eyes and make huffing noises, pacing back and forth on the balls of my feet, annoyed at my own inability to make a decision. I had to do the right things or I would totally screw myself. A desperate attempt to remember the Noble Eightfold Path became a broken mantra. Right view, right intention . . . right action . . . no. Right mindfulness? Right concentration, right living . . . what the hell were the last two? Right . . . right . . . right speech, and right . . . knowledge.

Yes. Those were it. Right speech and right knowledge.

I thought about the sum of my knowledge.

I said, “Fuck.”

What do I know? I know what a participle is. I know about the life and work of Immanuel Kant. I know which cashier is the nicest at the closest grocery store. I know how to crochet a scarf. I know how long to microwave popcorn for the most pops and the least kernels (the 'popcorn' button is a lie). I can thread a needle and get soap scum out of a shower. I know how to perform CPR. In theory.

I have extensive knowledge of the history of the Riot Grrrl movement and I know how to paint little skulls on my fingernails. I can also wax my own legs. I know where to find elusive items like mascara for redheads, a Korean-made bleaching toothpaste that actually works, and quality stockings with modest price tags. I know 65 Women's-Health-Magazine-recommended ways to keep the sex interesting in a long-term relationship and I know how to lose ten pounds in ten days.

I have a feeling that last one is going to be the most useless of all.

Personal dignity tells me that I know how to change a car tire, use jumper cables, shoot a gun, catch fish, start a fire, and pump my own gas, but I can't exactly guarantee these things from what you might call experience. But these are things that any idiot can do, right? People do them all the time. Someone, somewhere, is probably doing them right now.

The variation on the old joke is, "What do you do with a B.A in philosophy?" "Serve coffee." At the moment, there didn't seem to be anybody around who wanted coffee. I guess, post-Suck, what you do with a B.A. in philosophy is think. Most of the time, I'd rather think than serve coffee, anyway.

After these two ideas had passed, they bumped into each other again in the back of my brain. Suddenly all I wanted in the world was a cup of really awful corner-store coffee. I'd stopped drinking coffee years ago and swapped it out for tea, but I was thinking a little less clearly now that life had taken an incomprehensible nose dive. Coffee would make it okay. If I had coffee, it would be three years ago and none of this would be happening. Coffee, coffee, coffee. If only I could go to the store and get some awful coffee. If only I wasn't scared to go back outside.

Down the hall seemed safe enough, so I did a totally unconvincing Super Brave Power Walk to my neighbor's open apartment. It took me a full minute of mousy 'hello's' and hesitant shave-and-a-haircut knocking to talk myself two feet inside the door, but as soon as I did, there it was: Glorious coffee, right on the kitchen counter. I had the coffee. Everything was going to be okay.

I looked around their apartment and, with the nearly identical floor plans, this vacated mock-up of a Place to Live made me think of what my place would look like if I disappeared like the neighbors. My poor home . . . empty, dark, and perfectly still . . . all alone in the world.

I ran back to my apartment to keep it company, clutching the coffee. When I got back in, I spun on the linoleum in my hurry to lock the door. I wasn't going to leave my home to become a vacated freak show like the one down the hall. After checking each room to make sure they were still warm, full of stuff, and generally accounted for, I returned my attention to the coffee, which of course turned out to be in bean form. I had a grinder, but no power. Finally I just put the coffee bag inside a canvas bag and crushed it repeatedly with a wine bottle, which more or less did the trick.

It's probably for the best that I no longer owned a coffee maker, or I would have had one more chance to feel stupid and curse the lack of electricity. Instead, I heated up some water over the candles and dunked the coffee in it. The result was barely passable, but I tried to make it seem better by putting it in my favorite cup and setting it in a saucer that had spent six months as a water catcher for an African Violet. When I realized what I was doing, I sat down in front of my book/trophy shelf and started giggling.

My hard-earned B.A was on the middle shelf, still new enough that I'd propped it open front and center so I could feel accomplished. I was also still trying to process that this was a $125,000 piece of paper. I'd been through seven kinds of hell to get this inky thing, the only special properties of which were a small tin foil stamp and a bragging right.

Still giggling and bordering on hysterics, I put the saucer back under the African Violet and put my coffee down on the B.A's green leather binder. Eventually, the laughter cycled itself down to a few leaking tears and an occasional snorting noise. As I sat cross-legged in front of my bookshelf, holding my saucer-degree and letting the coffee cool, my face went from manic to meditative.

What do you do with a Philosophy degree?

Serve yourself coffee. Thoughtfully.

Books on my shelf at Time of Suck:

A Modest Proposal, by Jonathan Swift
All That Is Solid Melts into Air, by Marshall Berman
Bossypants, by Tina Fey
The Handmaid's Tale, by Margaret Atwood
The Hollow Chocolate Bunnies of the Apocalypse, by Robert Rankin
Looking for Alaska, by John Green
Notes from the Underground, by Fyodor Dostoyevsky
Sacre Bleu, by Christopher Moore
Skinny Legs and All, by Tom Robbins
St. Lucy's Home for Girls Raised by Wolves, by Karen Russell

Every time I went into a bookstore, I walked by hundreds of books on herb gathering, wilderness survival, animal behavior, car repair, first aid, edible mushrooms, and candle-making. There were entire sections for gardening and camping. For all I knew, carrot seeds come from little packets at the grocery store. I'd never even thought about it. I walked by all of those useful subjects, and what did I buy? *The Hollow Chocolate Bunnies of the Apocalypse.* I liked that book very much, but it furthered my functionality as a human being exactly one one-hundredth of one whit, and I'm only giving it that much credit because it contains a reminder not to fall into pits full of spikes.

Upon investigation, my closet proved to be a similar situation. Mankind created waterproof Gor-Tex steel-toed 12-eyelet mining boots, and, faced with hours to kill in a shoe store, I selected strappy purple Mary Janes.

Soon, I'd created a giant pile of clothing in the middle of my bedroom and started kicking it in frustration. I distinctly remembered buying clothes that were both practical and attractive. What happened to them? And where did all of this total shit come from? A sweater is supposed to be a heavy, wooly bundle of awesomeness that keeps you warm, isn't it? I'd always thought of some of these things as sweaters. So what are they, really, and why can I see through them? And while we're demanding information concerning my wardrobe, why are all my 'denim' pants made of the same stretchy junk as my dollar-store dish towels? Why did having a smiling cat printed on this fabric ever influence me to buy socks that start to disintegrate after ten or twelve wearings? Why don't any of my pants have real pockets? And last but certainly not least, why the HELL did I ever buy a skirt that I cannot even walk down a flight of stairs in?

Unfortunately, I know the answers to some of these questions. And to the last, if I recall, the answer is, "Because it makes my ass look like I work out, even though I don't." I suppose that bit of absurdity hints at what some of the other reasons may be.

Speaking of working out, being all alone in the world eventually points out how lame you got once you stopped riding your bike and using the campus gym. If you need proof of this, go to a room. Try to move the heaviest piece of furniture from one end to the other. On the off-chance that you succeed, your next task is to go throw a car in neutral and push it uphill. There are many physical tasks that people can accomplish with other people. I've helped to move stalled cars, bring queen-sized mattresses up stairs, and carry fellow human beings. We are like bees. We have the power of the hive.

In the first few days of being alone, I discovered that, all by myself, I can lift about sixty pounds and do three and a half push-ups.

Oh, yes. And I can tip over the refrigerator.

So far, I had some minimal and mostly perishable food, a bathtub full of water, some clothes that were barely designed to withstand the washing machine, and a body conditioned by years of drinking and holding down the couch to spring into action only if action required less than sixty pounds of lifting and could give me two or three hours to get started in the morning. This was not encouraging.

It suddenly seemed that the only useful thing I'd done with my life was develop a compulsive candle-buying habit. I had bags of tea lights. Scented jar candles from apple to vanilla were packed together on the windowsills. The centerpiece of my kitchen table was a small pewter candelabra, and there were colored taper candles for every mood or theme in the cupboard. Weird but irresistible impulse-buy candles, the kind of novelty candle I'd never burn, had been relegated to the bathroom shelves: Wax cats, dusty cartoon characters, a tiny hand-made one shaped like a vase of flowers that looked a little like a cartoon bomb. Thanks to the candle and incense addictions, I had lighters in every room as well. Matches populated the back of the silverware drawer, probably forming their own secret societies and plotting a war against the evil dust bunnies. Regardless of the possible secret lives of matchbooks, I was set for light and even a little heat.

The final inventory of everything else made me realize that sooner or later I'd have to go outside, so I started trying to work through my leaving-the-house routine.

Step one: Cover self in appropriate clothing for the occasion.

I spent fifteen minutes shifting through my pile of clothes looking for my suit of armor, which obviously I did not have, before giving up and going to sleep for ten hours.

Wake up. Try again.

Step one: Cover self in appropriate clothing for the occasion.

During the selection process, minor delays included yelling at my clothes pile, crying, attempting to put on everything at once, and screaming while throwing a useless see-through scrap of a shirt out the window, having been offended by the fact that it couldn't keep a Chihuahua warm in a Florida winter. I eventually selected a gray button-down shirt, black cargo pants (my only pair), and a spiked collar that made me feel safer for no good reason. Getting paranoid that I'd get stuck outside at night, layer after layer of socks suddenly seemed necessary. The addition of a pleather jacket made the whole thing look more sturdy, even if pleather is really about as protective as a ballet slipper.

At least I didn't have to resort to actual ballet slippers. Converse hi-tops would have to do.

Step two: Manage hair, add make-up, choose earrings, and take measures to smell socially acceptable.

No.

Step three: Gather material possessions required for the outing.

My candle-hoarding wasn't going to help me on this one. The good news was, my purse already contained a treasure trove of useful stuff. I find this is true of many purses. Common items include aspirin, antihistamines, tweezers, Band-Aids, tampons, eye drops, note books, mirrors, Chapstick, and travel items up to and including toothbrushes. I had all of these. Also, my giant ring of key-chain trinkets, acquired over years of boredom in check-out lines with help from the Christmas tradition of trying to fit gifts into a tiny sock, included not only miniature rubber ducks but also a miniature flashlight, a panic button, a tiny folding knife, and one of those screwdriver key things. These, it should be noted, are just the side pocket items. The main pocket of my purse already contained a paperback, two granola bars, a bag of potato chips (edible even in their crushed powder form), and three butterscotch candies. Add a water bottle and I'm ready to go hiking. Or to the bar. Either way.

The tradition of Grabbing the Purse also includes making a big loop of the house, carrying your bag in front of you in case any more useful items want to jump in. This time, the house loop garnered a cell phone, a water bottle, and the biggest knife in my kitchen. It wasn't a machete, but since all I was really hoping to do was scare off the more half-hearted sort of looter, it would probably do. As an afterthought, I added my glasses: Wouldn't want to lose a contact lens in this brave new world and walk off a cliff that wasn't there yesterday. I stopped with my hand on the door knob and went back for my Epi-pen. You never know. The major geological shift may have pissed off the bees.

When I started my moped, thirty seconds of emotional roller coaster ensued. Normally, it sounds like strangling duck, but the rain had stopped, and when the 49-cc engine fired up and echoed off the house, it put me in mind of a Boeing 747 taking off. Someone could hear me and find me. For a minute, I almost gunned it out of the driveway with joy: I could use this stupid bike as a signal! Someone would hear it! Someone would find me!

Then that first thought, a ride down the river of exhilaration, went over the waterfall. Someone will find me. Someone will find me and I have no control over who that someone might be. Some psycho killer will find me.

I hadn't even finished the thought before I killed the moped's keening-duck engine and leaped off the bike. In one little flash of insight, my precious moped had gone from a whirring savior to a sly banshee that would draw in any lurking danger and then putter away like a joke when I tried to flee. Twenty miles per hour was plenty to get the Cherry Garcia home from the grocery store before it melted; it would not be sufficient to escape a bear, or a landslide, or a person with a gun, or whatever completely horrible thing I was about to encounter.

That was the first time something snapped in me. It was a minor mental fracture, a miniature nervous breakdown, lasting less than a minute. It was probably completely normal. Stress does strange things to people.

That day, I spent the better part of a minute curled up in a ball, crying because everything was terrible and my moped didn't love me anymore.

For five minutes after that, I huddled against the side of my apartment building, staring into space and wondering what the hell just happened.

Then, I walked.

I used to think I had "normal" pinned down. It turned out that my previously-held definition was pretty narrow.

Before The Suck, I thought that seeing snow fall on Portland in early November was weird. It wasn't. Now, thinking I was looking at snow and realizing that it was volcanic ash . . . that was weird.

Twenty paces from my house, looking turned into seeing. Believing was delayed to thirty paces, the last ten of which decreased in speed until I was just standing on the sidewalk with one foot stuck out in the air. Ash. There is volcanic ash falling from the sky. The small amount of white flakes blowing gently down my block is not seed fluff or snow. The ground was still pretty clear, which was almost a shame, because there's nothing like a view of your own street being in each and every way subtly wrong to mess with you. The fire hydrants were open. The corner store looked just fine, other than the fact that it had gone dark. There was a bicycle chained to a signpost, but they were both mangled. Finally I realized that I could see all the way down the street. There was not one car. Never before had there been so much unoccupied curb in

Northeast Portland.

Scanning my brain for the keywords "What to do in case of volcanic ash" provided no results. It was not the kind of thing they had taught in New York public schools or even Portland colleges. It was probably somewhere in one of those piles of books I'd ignored at Powell's on my way to the textbook section, because *Skepticism 101* was so much more important than *What To Do In Case of Volcano.* Sometimes hindsight makes you want to hit yourself in the face with a stick.

I would have to come up with my own solution. I was a logical, functional human being. I knew how to use inductive and deductive reasoning, and apply the scientific method to everyday life. So of course, my first thought was "Hat. I should get a big hat."

I ran home. I stayed there for three days.

Here's a useful piece of information about bathtubs in lousy old apartment buildings: They leak. After fleeing from the volcano dandruff, the plan was to stay in my apartment forever. Good plan, right? Well, no. Of course not.

Day one was spent sleeping and putting all the useful items in my apartment in a big pile on the kitchen table, because staring at it made me feel better.

Day two was almost entirely occupied with sleeping. It was the kind of dull sleep symptomatic of post-break-up depression. As a matter of fact, I think that's exactly what it was. Earth had broken up with humans. The Sunday crossword, fast food cheeseburgers, karaoke, and frisbee in the park had all dumped my ass. There wasn't enough consolation ice cream in the world. Seeing as the power had been out for almost a week, there may not be any ice cream at all. Anywhere. Ever again.

Oh, god. Oh, god, everything is terrible. Oh, god and goddess and flying spaghetti monster and robot overlords, please give unto me a gun and the skills necessary to shoot myself in the head.

I thought about eating every pill in my medicine cabinet before realizing that I didn't really want to die, I just wanted to almost die because then someone would save me, which no one would, even if I ate every pill in the medicine cabinet.

God damn everything.

I did some form of mutant kickboxing workout to try to make myself feel better. Endorphins raised, I went about binge-eating the last of the food because it was all about to go bad. Well, mostly because it was about to go bad. I ate the Nutella just because I wanted it.

When I went to get some liquid refreshment out of the bathtub, I discovered that thing about lousy old apartment buildings: They leak.

The water level was down to a few inches. The next frantic half-hour was spent scooping my remaining supply into empty wine bottles and sun-tea jars. There didn't seem to be a way to get the last little puddle around the drain, so I just stuck my head in the tub and slurped it like soup. Then I stared at my useful stuff pile for a while and went back to bed.

Day three started out with many thoughts about water. I peed in a jar and refused to think about why I put a lid on it and hid it under the table.

In theory, I could make a rain-catching rig with some pretty basic household supplies, but it wasn't raining. It was ashing. Even if the falling dust was minimal, and even if it had been raining buckets (Oh, what I wouldn't have given for it to be raining buckets, preferably with water in them), I still didn't want to drink the tiniest bit of volcanic residue more than necessary. Unfortunately, this narrowed my options to A) Dying of dehydration, which I was pretty sure sucked and was slow, B) Drinking my own pee, or C) Going back outside. There was a resolute certainty in my mind that going back outside was the worst thing ever. Held up against the other two, though, it started to look a little better.

Most situations can be brightened when held up in the blinding metaphorical light of drinking your own pee. I didn't even have to try it to know how awful it was going to be. There's something instinctual about it. Looking at a jar of your own pee makes the body go, "No. You already drank that once. Don't do it again."

I found myself repeating empowering mantras that I'd picked up in my years of exposure to the internet. Rosie the Riveter under the words, "My balls are so big they had to go on my chest." Gloria Steinem saying "Some of us are becoming the men we wanted to marry." Getting all indignant about opening my own fucking pickle jar, thank you very much. It might have helped a little. The thing that helped the most was probably just *being thirsty.*

Better to stop trying to psych myself up and just do it. I added one more step to my pre-house-leaving checklist:

Step four: Cover self very, very well.

I added a black beret, sunglasses, and umbrella to my now super-fashionable outfit. On my way out the door, I wrapped my thin white scarf around my face. Now there was some chance of being able to breathe without sucking in any more volcano flakes.

Slowly and quietly, holding my body to make it seem as small as possible, I went down the hall, down the stairs, and outside. My moped was waiting, but I still didn't dare take the screaming harpy with me and constantly give away my position in this creepy new world. There were two bicycles in the street: One mangled and chained to a post, and one locked to a bike rack. I didn't know the first thing about picking bike locks, so I walked.

Always one scary thought away from running back to my apartment, I did the Converse-shod creep along Prescott. The first crow to make a little 'wrauk' sound at me made me jump behind a recycling bin. The second one made me freeze. By the time I made it to Thirty-Third Avenue, I was replying to each 'wrauk' and 'chuurk' with a gleeful “Fuck you!” and a wave of my middle fingers.

There had definitely been some kind of evacuation, and I had missed it. There were a few remaining cars, but most of them were clearly the kind of junker that the owner was 'going to fix up someday.' Some of the houses in Alameda Ridge still had SUVs parked in the driveway. I couldn't help but picture those people trying to evacuate . . . “Oh, no, honey! If I drive the Mini, and you take the Hummer, who's going to drive the Range Rover? We can't possibly leave it behind and little Blaine only has a learner's permit!” Those poor, poor bastards. Maybe they should have asked one of the nice National Guardsmen to drive it for them. Maybe they were going to, but they couldn't find a decent, young, white male who called them 'sir' and 'ma'am.' Damn women and minorities, joining the National Guard.

Would it have been the National Guard? Maybe it was policemen, or firemen who came door-to-door. Maybe no one came at all, and I just missed the radio announcement by virtue of not having a stupid radio. It seemed unlikely. But if some uniformed crew or other went around knocking on doors and telling people to clear out, where the hell was I? I mean, okay, I don't have my name on my mailbox (I'll get around to it one of these years), and my moped wasn't exactly the same indicator of Someone Home that a real car would have been, and I hardly knew anyone in the city because I hadn't gotten around to socializing just yet, but . . . well, the point is, I had a door, damn it. Would it have killed them to knock?

At any rate, the population had gone and taken all the everyday cars with them. The only things left were the best of the worst and the worst of the best. And my moped, of course . . . the thing only got up to twenty-five miles an hour with a stiff wind at my back, but it ran, so I mentally crowned it the best of the best of the worst of the remaining vehicles in Portland and decided to tune it up and take it out as soon as I got home. It may attract scary people, or bears or something, but even my moped went faster than the average human and probably even most animals. It wouldn't outrun a bullet, but no mode of transportation was going to do that, anyway. Traveling on foot didn't guarantee that big bad scary things wouldn't find me. It just guaranteed that if a big bad scary thing did find me, I would be on foot. Now leaving my moped at the house seemed like a really stupid thing to do, but it was too late to go back for it.

I reached the end of the thought process around the same time I made it to Broadway.

My feet had auto-piloted my ass to the grocery store.

The giant, maze-like grocery and department store with no windows and no power.

Which would surely occur to any serial killers left around as a great place to stock up on axes.

Fuck my life.

I hid in the bottle return hut for a while, peeking over a grocery cart and plotting my next move. How do you break in to a department store? Brick through the glass door? Was there some kind of roof entrance? I gripped the shopping cart a little harder for each second that passed without a brilliant plan. My hands started shaking. Then the grocery store started shaking.

I discovered something about earthquakes that day: They are LOUD.

My brilliant plan suddenly came clear to me. It didn't involve breaking into the store. It involved getting as far as possible from the giant shaking metal bins full of glass that I was, at that moment, sharing the bottle return hut with. It was a good plan, and I went with it.

Since the nearest object was a sickly, unstable-looking tree, I ran most of the way across the parking lot to hold on to a cart corral. It was kind of sort of like a doorway, and I remembered that much about natural disasters: Earthquakes mean hiding in doorways.

I only fell over three times during that run. When the planet is shaking, let's see anyone else do better.

The quake lasted for less than thirty seconds.

Activity so intense for such a short period of time gives a girl two weird feelings in a row. First, after a few seconds, there is the realization that this is going to go on forever. Then, as soon as it stops, it never happened, because the brain didn't have the time to process it. Possibly this is some demonstration of how amazing the human brain is, adjusting and readjusting reality, plugging up potential crazy with a handy coping mechanism.

As for myself, I think it demonstrates that the human brain is made of recycled monkey bits and pure, unadulterated stupid.

This was verified when the aluminum post I was gripping popped right out of the ground and my first reflex was to try and shove it back in.

The shaking stopped. I was laying in the parking lot, curled up in a ball and clutching the pole from the cart corral for dear life, probably looking like some kind of demented post-apocalyptic stripper. I opened my eyes.

My first thought was not *I'm alive!* or *It's over!* It was *There is no graceful way to recover from this embarrassing position.* A lifetime of peer pressure was so effective that my response to a near-death experience was to feel like I'd been pantsed by the planet. At least there was no one around to witness my awkward survival.

Except there was still a loud rumbling noise. It didn't sound like the earthquake, or a landslide. It sounded like an engine.

When a person doesn't speak for a long time, it's almost like the body forgets how. When I tried to get the first word out, it was like having laryngitis and hangover mouth at the same time. Lame. Weak.

"Hello?"

Insufficient. Had to do something.

I started to stump across the parking lot towards the sound on whatever combination of limbs felt like working in a given step. Awkward-monkey-crawl turned into power-crab-jog. I was a poster child for the Ministry of Silly Walks.

"Hello!"

I rounded the corner of the building like a dog roller-skating on marbles. The truck was already turning on to Twenty-Eighth Avenue. I tried to chase it, but the functionality of my legs wasn't improving and the thin layer of ash had stuck to the ground here, behind the store and out of the wind. By the time I got to Twenty-Eighth and Broadway, it was gone.

Who were they? Looters? A zombie-apocalypse-style

survival crew? (What's the difference, again?) Suddenly it seemed possible that chasing a truck full of total strangers was maybe not such a good idea. Surviving gangs in fiction were always plucky pals trying to get by and do good in a world gone mad. A college education in the history of the world, especially as seen through the lens of philosophical studies, presents a different picture. Surviving gangs were probably comprised of sociopaths. Thieves, at the very least. If they weren't killers yet, it wouldn't be long in the cold wind that was lack of civilization before the hard moral lines got blurry. If I ran into people and they stole my purse, that would be bad. But there was also a greatly increased chance that they would kill me, which would obviously be worse.

But there was that chance of rescue. Of strangers evacuating me to some massive shelter in the Rose Quarter. Feeding me. These things were possible, too, but the brain made of recycled monkey bits wouldn't give strangers the benefit of the doubt, no matter how many persuasive arguments I had. There were scary people around. There might still be scary people in Aisle 6, too, and if I went back for the pasta and canned pears like I'd originally planned, they would kill me.

It's very hard to re-train the higher brain functions to believe in dangers like that after a lifetime of relative safety.

Someone could kill me. Not 'give me a fright.' Not 'be all menacing.' Not 'accidentally bruise my shoulder in karate class.' Kill me. With their hands. On purpose. There wouldn't be an intervening old lady calling the cops, or an ambulance. I would not wake up in a hospital having survived a harrowing ordeal. I would not post about it on Facebook and draw a full month of sympathy out of my friends. If someone tried to kill me here, now, I would just die. Crows would probably eat me.

Maybe that was the way to go.

No, I thought. *Let's not start that deathwish shit again.*

At the corner of Twenty-Eighth and Broadway, there is a pet store. In the window of that pet store, there are cats.

Cats are independent, resourceful animals, possibly these more than most. They were rescues from the Oregon Humane Society, currently living on their lives on public display because some crafty person had realized that people were more likely to spontaneously take a cat home from the window of a pet store than wander in to an animal shelter. These lucky kitties would have been on their way to good homes, if there had been any good homes left.

Now, instead of a loving family and a mouse-infested basement to play in, they were stuck with a wire mesh cage and a quickly diminishing supply of food.

And me. Staring in the window at them.

My face blurred in the dirty glass. The reflection wobbled like a funhouse mirror as I shifted from foot to foot. The cats ignored me.

I didn't know how to break in to a pet store any more than I knew how to pick the bike lock or raid the grocery store, but at least this had big windows. The earthquakes hadn't even touched them.

It is entirely possible to break a window, but it's not as easy as it looks in the movies. I didn't have any half-bricks handy. The knife in my purse wasn't exactly a fire ax. And I couldn't rip a signpost out of the ground. Hell, if I could rip a sign post out of the ground, I probably could have just put my fist through the window, instead. Maybe kicking it was the solution.

I knew how to properly execute a roundhouse kick

because one of the things to do as a female college student in a big scary new city is take self-defense classes. It's an extracurricular so common that it might as well be a law.

The glass was a more fearsome opponent than the training bags. If a person hurts themselves on a training bag, it was because they were sloppy and clenched their fist too soon, or let their ankle go slack. If a person hurts themselves breaking glass, it's because . . . well, it's *glass*, stupid. Glass is one of those thing we're taught very early in life not to fuck with, like fire or electricity. Glass will bite. Glass is bad. We never think about it, walking down the street with giant panes of the stuff on all sides, but one little exertion of force and glass becomes very dangerous.

I took a fighting stance against the window and raised my right leg, folded it at the knee. Then I put it back down. Things were starting to come clear. The new reality was cracking through the old habit, and the new reality was that a little boo-boo could end my whole miserable life. Staph infection. Tetanus. Bleeding out. I looked at my gritty reflection, tilted my head, and started taking off my jacket.

Taking clothing meant for the upper body and applying it to a foot is not easy. I was panicking that some poor cat was going to starve to death in the time it took me to wrap my stupid shoes in pleather. Then it came together. The arms of my jacket wrapped around the toe of my shoe three whole times. The collar flapped on my ankle like a superhero cape. I got back into my fighting stance and bounced up and down a few times, shaking out my nerves.

Leg up. Knee bent. Pivot the body. Snap the knee. Point the foot. Smash the window into quite a few large pieces. Hop back on one foot while the large pieces fall all over the place and turn into small pieces. Head back towards the window. Stop.

Luckily, I was starting to develop an eye for things that were about to kill me. A large triangle of glass was still vibrating at the top of the window. I backed up to watch it fall and shatter, then started kicking the smaller shards out of the frame. One more hazard avoided, I actually took the time to revel in my badassery. I just kicked in a window! I am queen bitch of awesome mountain! Look out, whatever's left of the world! I shook out my jacket and put it back on, dusting off the shoulders and feeling like I'd just leveled up. I could do anything. I was rough and tough and scary and a natural-born inanimate-object killer.

Time to rescue some kitties.

The gap from the departed window was nearly floor to ceiling, so instead of having to crawl through, I got to stride in like a video game cut-scene, plucking my jacket off of my foot and throwing it over my shoulder, hips swinging. I whipped off my sunglasses. It was amazing, right up until it was really sad.

There was a bright blue parakeet lying broken on the tile floor. I don't know how it got there. Maybe it escaped. Maybe it had lived its life as a sort of 'demo bird' that had free range of the store. Regardless, it appeared to have ended its little freelance domesticated existence by hitting the nearly mirror surface of a tarantula tank. My first thought was, *You, me, and the whole god damn world, you poor bastard.* Earth had caught a bad case of tarantism, and was trying to shake it off in the same way that frenzied dancing was once thought to cure the spider's bite. The Planetary Tarantella.

There was a blue and white feather stuck to the side of the spider tank. The tarantula was scrabbling at the side, trying to get to it.

I didn't know what I was supposed to do with a dead parakeet, but I found a small birdcage, filled the bottom with cedar shavings, and buried the bird in it. As I stretched to put the cage up high, to ensure some peace for the tiny bundle of feathers, I wondered if it was really any good to bury a bird in a cage. I wish I could have set it free somehow, even if it was too late, but I did the only thing that seemed even remotely right. I left the cage door open.

Once the bird was taken care of, I opened about fifty cans of cat food and dog food and put them on the sidewalk in front of the window. I poured a ten-pound bag of birdseed the length of the block. I opened every kind of rat, mouse, chinchilla, ferret, and hamster food and flung them to the four winds across the street. Looking around for any supplies that might be helpful to a human, I found a few items but nothing that exactly constituted a survival kit. The dog food was tempting, but I wasn't sure I could stand to eat the colorless wobbly bits, so I grabbed two bags of all-natural nuts and seeds meant for parrots and stuffed that in my purse instead. Then I opened a third bag to eat immediately.

Chowing down on a bag of peanuts and dried red peppers instantly brought to my attention how incredibly thirsty I was. My eyebrows shot up as my tongue turned into a disgusting, constricting piece of salted muscle in my mouth. For a second, I thought I'd accidentally eaten some kind of dehydrated sardine, but it was, in fact, my tongue. I needed water immediately.

I lifted the hanging water bottle out of a gerbil cage and spent a few seconds trying to figure out how the hell to use the roller ball and drink from it before just unscrewing the top. A quarter cup of water was enough to rehydrate my tongue. There was a mild burning sensation that I tried to convince myself was refreshing. A person can't live long without water, but even a small amount can change your whole body. When in desperate need, a little water can feel like a medication, a shower, and a belly full of sweet tea all at once.

The gerbil I'd cadged water from was looking at me. It had big shiny black eyes and a quivering little nose. It radiated a passive-aggressive guilt trip about what I had just done. I looked down at it.

"Sorry, buddy."

I lifted it out of the big glass tank and set it free. It was probably a hell of a lot better at finding water than I was, anyway.

A spice finch beside me let out an experimental chirrup, and suddenly the collective birds started up their collective and varied calls in their cages, the avian "Bohemian Rhapsody." Can domestic birds fly? Don't pet stores clip their wings or something? The little finches and canaries seemed to be flitting through the air without much trouble. I opened the cages. Nothing happened. Then, one intrepid zebra finch landed on the door to the cage and started running through that strange head-tilting routine that looks like they're trying to recalibrate their own brain. With one last 'werk' noise, it took off.

Gone! A feathered exodus winged it out of the pet shop, following the leader. Not all of them flew well, but hopping from cages to counters, they all made it.

When I opened the cages of the larger birds, they seemed far less inclined to go. An elderly parrot regarded me with one shining black and gold eye. Eventually, I reached in to touch it and it stepped up on to my finger. With minimal effort I managed to transfer it to my shoulder. Soon I was wearing a collection of parrots, parakeets, and cockatoos like a living feather boa. They rustled when they moved. One stuck a feather in my ear as it tried to preen. Slowly, I shuffled my way across the shop and stepped out of the broken window. The birds on my arms and shoulders stayed put. One of them said "Brrrk."

I looked down the street, both ways, and listened hard, trying to make sure there was no one else around. I was still alone.

Not sure what else I expected, really, but at least it freed me up to execute the next step.

Draining the gerbil's water bottle had helped clear my throat a little. The falling ash had decreased, now more like a dollar-store snow globe than a Claymation Christmas special, so I was able to take a good, deep breath.

I screamed.

The birds took off.

The fish were trickier. I couldn't exactly release them down the street drains. Fortunately, there were two large display tanks in the pet store, one for fresh and one for salt water. I transferred all the fish into the appropriate tank, hoping that with the live plants and the plecos there would be a sufficient mix to form a little ecosystem. In the tanks, too, went a large supply of fish food and some pirate-themed ceramic sculptures. A laughing buccaneer skull drifted to the bottom of the freshwater tank. The fish had gone rogue. They were now free bandits of the low seas.

Then I turned back to the cats.

There were six cats in a large, multi-tiered metal cage. Three were a nondescript grey with stripes, the sort of universal cat shape and size where I'd see two walking around the neighborhood and be convinced that they were the same cat until I saw both of them together. One was a small tuxedo-kitty with a white patch exactly where a Van

Dyke should be. This made me emit a little 'Eeeee' sound (Even in the middle of a global disaster, kittens are still cute). Two were orange and extremely fluffy. These were curled up together in a cat bed, looking like one poof-tastic mutant creature.

The cage was very simple. There were no locks, just sliding latches. I set the cats free.

But first, I freed all the rodents, and I gave them a head start.

While I emptied a shelf of bird food into a large re-usable canvas bag, I thought about the other things a person is supposed to have in case of emergency. Flashlights. Rope. A battery-powered radio. A generator. A long list of other stuff that I was unlikely to find in a pet store. However, a few substitutions could be made. I felt pretty silly putting leashes and light-up collar charms in my bag, but at least I had them.

A sort of utility dog collar also presented itself. There was a picture of a dog hiking with a human on the package. The collar itself had a tiny water bottle, a few pouches for treats, a few D-rings and an adjustable buckle. I couldn't bring myself to actually put it around my neck (there's that old Pre-Suck thinking again . . . what if I was wearing that and somebody *saw* me?), but I found that when I tightened it around my thigh it held itself up just fine. Now I had a utility garter.

I filled the miniature water bottle from another one in the former chinchilla cage. There wasn't anything that seemed useful small enough to fit in the pouches. As an afterthought, I picked a large spiked collar off the leash rack and tightened it around my other thigh. It was almost a small piece of armor. Also, it made me feel less silly about wearing the utility collar on the other leg.

Just when I thought the pet store had provided everything useful it could, I spotted the corded phone on the counter. Cell phones might be dead, but landlines were a good, strong old-school system. I picked up the handset. To my complete disbelief, there was a dial tone. I stopped breathing for three whole seconds. Finally, I dialed 911.

Ring. Click. Ring.

Click.

Ring.

Click.

Forever and ever, amen.

Balls.

Outside the pet store, I popped open my umbrella and turned left. There were still no signs of people, but there were plenty of signs that people had *once been*. The gas station at Twenty-Fifth was flying a sign that said "Closed. Out of Gas. Sorry." Even the emergency lights were out, but I could see inside well enough to tell that someone had raided the place. I hope it was some enterprising employee who loaded up on chips, jerky, beer, and cigarettes before getting the hell out of Dodge. Here was yet another way that being unemployed had screwed me: No work place to steal from.

There was an auto shop a little further down the road with the garage bay open. I checked it out from behind a lamp post. So far, out of a thousand fears of encountering another living thing, nine hundred and ninety-nine had been unjustified, and the one time that there had been someone in sight, I'd forgotten my fear and chased them down the street only to lose them. Still, I watched the garage and waited. Just in case.

No one was there. I called another creaky "Hello?" when I got to the bay door.

A squirrel ran out.

I went in.

There was a vending machine in the office. There may not be much to be said in the nutrition category for sugary puffed rice, but I could swear I never needed anything so badly in my entire life. I leered at it until my forehead clonked against the cool Plexiglas. The sound it made was the starting buzzer of the next puzzle: How to get goodies out of a vending machine when the power was out. *Thwok*. Go.

Logical step one was the smash the front. I found a decent-sized spanner, which looked huge in my tiny hands, and gave the front plate a few experimental whacks. No dice. There was, I admit, some temptation to just sit down in front of the machine and cry.

Why couldn't just one thing be simple? Why didn't anything work anymore? Ahh!

It wasn't that the vending machine wouldn't give up the edibles. It was that this was the millionth thing in a row that just wouldn't go my way. There comes a point when a person just wants to give up and go back to bed. I couldn't do that, but no matter how mature we get or how sensible we think we are, there's some bit of brain that is always susceptible to having a hissy fit in the conviction that this will result in some food, a good comforting, and a nap.

In this case, I had to settle for muttering "*Damn*," and looking for logical step two.

I tossed the spanner and rummaged around the shop until I found a crowbar. Then I climbed up on top of the vending machine and jammed it into the little crack between the front plate and the rest of the machine. After a few minutes of wriggling, chipping, and kicking, there was a loud crack, and the cornucopia of sugar and salt opened to me. I ate a rice crispy treat right there on the oily floor of the auto shop. An empty brake pad box served to carry the rest.

Now I had too much stuff. I had to take it back to the house before I found something else useful and had to start dragging things on a sled (not that I had a sled). Still no water, though. Not in any meaningful amount. I started mumbling again.

"*Of course there's no water, why keep that shit around when it comes out of the sink? It falls from the sky! It covers most of the planet! Who needs it! Ha. Hahaha . . . stupid.*"

It was a problem for later. Right now, I had to figure out how to carry all this junk and keep the falling ash off at the same time. Several experiments were made and I dropped the box of vending machine food twice, the second time losing a package of cashews down a storm drain. With the scarf back over my face, breathing hard and sweating a little, I almost started to feel claustrophobic. In the end, I stuck the umbrella down the back of my jacket and piled all my goodies on top of the brake pad box to carry in front of me, though seeing over the stack was nearly impossible. It would have to do.

I started the long walk home, passing the tuxedo cat on the street with a polite nod.

What would have been nice, I thought, *was someone to help me carry all this food. I'd even be willing to split it.*

I knew I wasn't the last person on Earth, but my trusty gang of zombie-fighting misfits had somehow failed to materialize. I had to assume that most people went, "Fuck! I'm in a major metropolitan area! This is where the bad stuff always happens in the movies!" There were probably people hiding in their basements, counting their canned goods, too. Walking through seemingly empty neighborhoods on my way back to my house made me wonder about the possibilities of people still being in the houses. Halfway home, I sat down on the brake pad box and looked up the street. Could I believe that there was no one left? That people who need people were the unluckiest people in the world? I was almost desperate enough to start knocking on doors. What would make people answer? I retreated completely into my own head as I picked up my box and trudged on.

List of possible things to yell in a desperate door-to-door companion search:

"FEMA!"
"Trick or Treat!"
"Mostly Harmless!"

Maybe I should make a survivalist-team-member resume to give out, in case I should meet anyone.

Mab.
24.
Female.
140 lbs.
College Graduate (Philosophy)

Skills:
Crochet
Making tea
Amateur piano playing
Snarky blogging

Hm.
I should not make a resume.

Rounding the corner of Thirty-Third and Fremont, I heard a sound so common that I failed to register it for a full five seconds. There was a dog barking.

The box was heavy. I was taking any excuse to put down my pile of pseudo-groceries and shake the feeling back into my arms. A dog was good enough. Taking the crowbar with me, I started scouting around.

I finally found the source of the bark in the window of a house down the block. He was a big dog, some kind of extra-fluffy mutt, frantically making noise and weaving back and forth like he was working up the nerve to leap straight off the couch and through the glass. For a minute, I was very upset. Who leaves their dog locked up in the house when they're evacuated?

Then again, there were perfectly reasonable explanations. Maybe these people weren't home when it all happened. Maybe they had been off visiting family in a place that was now underwater, or underground. Maybe their friend was supposed to watch the house for them but got stuck south of Powell. I went from hating people to missing people desperately in the course of three thoughts. The dog continued to go nuts.

I used the crowbar to open a window. The dog jumped out and ran off. *Oh, well,* I thought, *At least he isn't going to get hit by a car.* I listened to him bark until he was out of earshot and left an open bag of cheese crackers on the ground in case he tried to come back for food. My job here was done.

Except there might be something to drink in the house. It had to be empty or someone would have either called out to me or hushed the dog so I wouldn't find them. I called "Hello?" through the window, just in case, then thought that if 'hello' came out of my mouth one more time in a row today I might as well go back and join the parrots from the pet store, who were probably nesting in the stop lights by now. I climbed in the window. My shoe caught on a painted nail, but I tore it free and tumbled onto the carpet in a pile of flailing limbs and dust.

The smell inside the house made me want to climb right back out again. With the power out, the people gone, and trash pick-up canceled indefinitely, nature was taking liberties with anything biodegradable that had been left inside. If Rot were personified, his slimy ass would now be laughing in the face of preservatives. It was the kind of smell against which ceasing to breathe was barely a defense, because you could feel it burning your eyes and getting in through your ears. There was no way in hell I was going to open that refrigerator.

There was a closet open in the shadowy kitchen. The dog had pawed his way into it and shredded the dog food bag, but had also revealed some warm bottles of flavored water on a shelf. I grabbed a red shopping bag from a hook, stuffed them in, and reverse-Santa-Claused it out of the house.

Finally, I crossed into my own neighborhood with my giant pile of stuff. When I turned on to Prescott Street, I found a hole in it. There was, in fact, more of the hole than there was of Prescott. I felt my stomach drop into my shoes as I smelled the broken sewer line and heard a distant clattering noise, like someone throwing an armload of two by fours into the bed of a truck.

The last earthquake had shifted my neighborhood, and it had all been slowly keeling over into Prescott Street ever since. I watched as the last of my porch fell off.

My moped, despite the dual kickstand, had rolled into the street and was leaning over the edge of what was now the beginning of Prescott Canyon. I dropped all my new supplies and ran in to rescue it. It was a stupid thing to do, but sometimes a lady has to do the stupid thing and hope. This time it worked. The soft rubber grips of the handlebars stuck to my palms as I twisted and yanked the machine back from the edge of oblivion. I panted. It creaked. I fought harder, and gravity let it go my way.

I righted the moped, started it, and puttered to the safety of a neighbor's yard where the ground seemed more stable. Then I spent the next half-hour watching my house finish the slow, thunderous collapse that had started in my absence. In the end, most of it slid into the hole in the street.

That was the last event of the Great Suck. Others can call it as they will, but that's where it ended for me, because after that, the universe could do no worse.

CHAPTER TWO
FOOD, WATER, SHELTER

I am not homeless. I am a free-spirited gypsy traveler whose only roof is the sky and whose alarm clock is the chattering of angry, angry squirrels.

I am not hungry. I am engaged in a spiritually cleansing separation from the modern consumerist culture of gluttony and entitlement.

I am not thirsty. I am . . . .fuck it. I am so, so thirsty.

Keeping a positive attitude when totally displaced means pretending to be someone else entirely. If I were in my post-Suck position and I were, say, Tank Girl, life would be pretty sweet. On the other hand, if I were just myself, then life is just me breaking into Port-a-Potties at construction sites because trying to pee out in the open gives me serious anxiety.

By the third day of being a free-spirited gypsy traveler engaged in a separation from modern consumerist culture, I had rewired my own brain to make me someone else, instead. Someone tougher. Someone who could live like this. I taught myself to yell "Pa-pa-pa-pow!" while urinating on signposts. Standing up.

Girls can do it, but it's tricky.

I learned a lot of things in those first few days, including many more reasons to wish that the stupid apocalypse had come in the form of zombies. If everyone turns into zombies, all the food, bottled water, camping supplies, and guns are just left lying around for the picking. Zombies are the Christmas morning of apocalypses, leaving mountains of gifts for the lucky, plucky survivors. But when people remain people, and those people leave, they take all that with them.

When I finally got up the nerve to go back to the grocery store, it was not the supply heaven I was hoping for. The bay door around back had been left open by the mysterious truck people I'd run after before, so getting in was easy, but the inside was like a cave. A big, boxy cave someone dug through a landfill. Not only was the produce growing its very own death-smelling mold crop, but everything that was left was junk.

In a normal, run-of-the-mill shopping day, people argued with themselves for fifteen minutes about what kind of pig product to take home and decided to get chicken instead because it was ten percent off. When the news starts airing a forecast of danger, though, everyone is suddenly running around scarfing up the same stuff. I remember seeing a study once that said top-sellers in pre-disaster times were beer and pop-tarts, and those things were certainly gone. As the news got scarier and people started leaving, that's when I imagine their priorities started straightening out. The aisle of canned goods had been reduced to a few dented tins on the top shelves that no one could see or reach without jumping. Camping gear had disappeared. Likewise auto supplies, over-the-counter medications, large plastic totes, and toilet paper. The only battery left in the Duracell display was the big cardboard one on top. Scouting around with my keychain flashlight, I found a large frame-pack in the decimated camping section and stuffed it with the scraps that the rest of humanity left behind on their way out: A child-size tent. Two tarps. Emergency space-blanket. Four cans of beans and a box of spaghetti. The last package of lemon-flavored Propel Zero. Travel packets of aspirin and generic cold/flu meds. The pharmacy had clearly been raided, but I noticed that there were still a few prescriptions in the recesses of the pigeonholes, organized and labeled and waiting to be picked up in their little white bags. One I recognized as an antibiotic. I didn't know what the rest of them were, but they all went into the backpack before I slunk out of the grocery-cave and back into the fresh air.

On a related note, I learned something that should have been self-evident: Books, movies, all kind of fictions, are full of lies. On the one hand, duh. But on the other hand, I've definitely watched someone in a movie climb a tree for safety and tie themselves in to sleep for the night, and I thought, *Hey, that would totally work.*

It didn't.

If you decide that you'd be safest in a big old maple, and you climb one, and you tie yourself to it . . . make sure you can untie the knots in the morning. I am almost certain that nearby squirrels were laughing at me.

This lesson cost me two hours of daylight and some bleeding fingers. It's obvious from the fact that I even tried it that the child-size tent didn't work out. I put my foot right through Dora the Explorer's plastic face.

Other lies from survival fiction:

Nurses, pilots, ex-military personnel, scientists, and

plain-spoken but good-hearted redneck hunters will come out of the woodwork until any survival crew has at least one of each. I'm calling bullshit based on two things: One, I hadn't actually seen a single other person, and two, if there was anyone out there, the only person I could guarantee they might find was me. My greatest skill so far was breaking into vending machines. The law of averages suggests that there's a whole lot more retail workers than brilliant geologists left in the world.

Many of my favorite books from childhood, where kids and teens get stranded in the wilderness and adapt to survive, tried to tell me that teaching yourself to hunt for food is something an eight-year-old can do without much difficulty. Later reading taught me that you can practically poison yourself if you don't know how to clean game properly. Still, I remember one of those kids learning to hunt ptarmigan, a camouflaged bird that freezes when threatened, by looking for the shape instead of the movement. Based on my experience, this is too good to be true. I don't think you just adapt to find invisible birds. I think you probably just scream each time one explodes out of the ground under your feet, and then you starve to death. Then, the ptarmigan eat you.

And last but certainly not least, there is no magical clear answer on what to do next. The brilliant geologist is not here to tell you, there is no rendezvous site from which the military will evac you, and there are no prophetic dreams. Well, maybe the brilliant geologist, the ex-military person, and Stephen King are somewhere out there, together, executing a well-thought-out Civilization Plan B and having prophetic dreams, but I didn't get any.

The last thing that I learned early on was about people.

By day four or five, I was still trying to piece together

a life. I'd started a makeshift camping site in Wilshire Park because the area didn't seem as affected by the minor earthquakes still hitting now and then, and just in case that changed, it seemed better to be outdoors. A roof over my head would have been nice, but I was no longer totally convinced that roofs were things that stayed where they were supposed to. Better to camp out than find myself getting too friendly with a ceiling. This considered, I was stringing up a tarp between three trees when I heard the noise.

Guns do not go 'pew.' In the unpopulated quiet, coming from a long way off, they sound like a lighting strike turning a tree into splinters.

A lot of synapses snapped together in my brain at the same time. *Gun. Guns don't go off by themselves, so that means people. People! Run towards the sound! People firing guns. Run away from the sound. Good people. Bad people. Schrodinger's people. Go find out what it was. Get as far away as possible. Stay right where I am and throw up because my stomach feels like a kiddie pool with a downed power line in it.*

The only one of those things I could do with any certainty was vomit. So I did that.

Then I headed down Thirty-Seventh, towards the noise, sneaking through back yards, because when it comes right down to it, I had to go. It's some back-end part of human nature to try and make the whole universe seen, known, and accounted for.

Outside the Wilshire Market, there was a dead man in the parking lot. His bright blue shirt had turned dark purple under him. He reminded me of the parakeet.

There was the faintest possible sound of a truck engine, headed away down Fremont Street. Just when it had almost faded for good, someone in that truck let out a loud, whooping laugh, like a Saturday night drunk about to turn into a Sunday morning problem. The sound of an evil sense of humor just waiting to happen to someone. That had already happened to someone.

It took me a full strung-out minute to convince myself there was nothing I could or should do. I couldn't bury him like I had done for the bird. I couldn't even have lifted him.

I ran back to the park.

Under stress, the human body has an unpleasant tendency to empty itself in every possibly way. We even built it right into our language, in phrases like 'so angry I could spit.' The need to pee will strike when it's least appropriate. When we're really freaking out, water just pours out of our faces, as well. And then, ladies and gentlemen, there is throwing up.

I have no idea why we evolved in such a way that our bodies believe vomiting is so helpful. The only thing I can think is that our far-distant ancestors, who stupidly ate the green berries or the red dirt, threw them back up like an acidic Technicolor Christmas and therefore lived longer. The body, however, extends this practice to offer it as the solution to any kind of stress or discomfort. When your biggest stress is about how little food and water you have, this becomes the dumbest mechanism there ever was. It's actually upsetting. After the Suck, vomiting was not only a bad idea but also a huge indignity on two levels. The first, true throughout history, was *Uhhhg, my body is doing something disgusting.* But the second, the really ridiculous indignity, was *Hey! I just ate that!* I needed that food, damn it, and my body was just tossing my hard-earned cookies without the least regard for my survival.

Of course, total bastard that the body is, the other thing it wants to do under stress is *eat.* I can't even speak for this being an evolved behavior. It might just be something that came from a lifetime of being told breakup = ice cream, personal success = cheesecake, and hangover = bacon.

Breakups, or even relationships, seemed unlikely to present themselves in my immediate future. Ice cream was also out of the question. The low-fat organic kind was probably the first to dissolve and mold when the power went out. Still, my body was having that firmly instituted reflex: Everything sucks! Eat food!

When the available food stash consists of a can of beans and half a box of spaghetti, this is bad advice. When one has a panic attack and throws up every time a branch cracks, it's even worse.

As a temporary measure, I broke into an already-raided gas station and took up smoking instead. There were two cartons of Misty menthol light 100's left under the counter. As a bonus, whoever had been there before me didn't seem to like anything barbeque-flavored, so I got away with a couple pounds of chips and some pork rinds. It was the best day since the Suck. Any day I was full of pork rinds was a good day, and smoking a cigarette made peeing on a lamp post while pretending to be Tank Girl all the more satisfying.

So far, I had been storing all my food in the frame pack and carrying it around with me. This was fine so long as my supply of edibles was minimal, but floating right on the surface of the part of my brain that evolved before opposable thumbs was the idea that *minimal food is bad.* I wanted *maximum food. All the food.* Having a stash that would last three days, provided I only engaged in enough physical activity to get more food, was bad. Even over the constant yammering of my higher brain functions, the endless litany of analyzing the new world, criticizing every step of my own behavior, and the panicky need to come up with a better plan, I could hear it. Pre-Suck, there had been a kitchen full of food, and the whole grocery store was available to re-stock it. Now the grocery store was a trash cave and my non-existent cupboards were almost bare. I didn't just need a few bags of barbeque chips. I needed a grocery store.

There had to be at least a hundred of them in Portland. Even subtracting fifty for the inaccessible and partially demolished west side of the river, that was still more than could possibly have been thoroughly cleaned out at evac time, or even in the post-evac raids I'd nearly run into. I started wracking my brain. Where the hell were the other ones?

I hadn't gone east of Wilshire Park by more than a couple of blocks. The next major nest of former human supplies would be out on Eighty-Second Avenue. Everything between was residential. The trip there would be long, and bringing myself to approach another source of supplies despite fear of encountering someone else's survival team would be difficult, but it was something to think about.

In the meantime, I had to find the best way to squirrel away my glorious new pile of barbeque-flavored goodies. I've been camping at state parks, and they say to hang food in a tree to keep it away from bears. I'm sure this is good advice. However, hanging a lifetime supply of pork rinds in a tree in a bright yellow reusable bag is not the best way to hide it from fellow humans, and there might now be someone out there who was willing to shoot a fellow human in the face for a bag of puffed salted pig parts. Since I did not want said fellow human to be me, I tried other arrangements.

Burying it occurred to me first. I didn't have a shovel, so I used the crowbar to break up the ground and then scooped it out with my hands. The hole was about two feet deep before I remembered: Bears. Or if not bears, then dogs, cats, crows, raccoons, skunks, or even squirrels. How deep do you have to bury something before a dog can't smell it anymore? I had a feeling that the answer was 'all the way.' Dogs could smell pork rinds if you'd eaten them three days ago. Dogs could dig like maniacs. Dogs could defend themselves with nothing but their built-in, natural weapons. Dogs were amazing, amazing creatures. I cursed them all as I filled in the hole. Even a hungry Chihuahua would be too much for me to face right now. Better to just do a sufficient job hiding the food.

I spent fifteen minutes sitting cross-legged, looking up, down, and all around while stuffing my face with half a bag of pork rinds. Where do you put things to keep them safe?

Two hours later, I chained a small antique safe from a used furniture store to my moped and dragged it halfway across town, struggling along at five miles an hour and throwing up sparks.

Then I buried it, door up, in the park. Kicking a layer of cedar chips over the top worked just fine. To celebrate, I ate the rest of that bag of pork rinds. Things were looking up.

Falling asleep that night, my mind started to glitch. When I'd really be drifting off, I'd think *I should go to the grocery store tomorrow*. Then I would wake myself up, annoyed, and think *You can't go to the grocery store tomorrow, stupid. It's closed. On permanent holiday. Empty*. And I'd try to remember where all the other grocery stores in Portland were, the ones I never went to because you pick a favorite and trudge the path back and forth from it for as long as you live there, stuck in your track.

There were other options, though, and I knew it. Even I, in a break from my grocery rut, would sometimes go all the way out just past Eighty-Second to a bulk foods store and buy a couple pounds of pistachios or a giant box of macaroni. Since moving to Portland I had tried to go vegetarian several times, and each time, when I gave up after less than a month, I would take that trip out to the bulk food store to stock up on chicken fingers, usually snagging a three-pound package of bacon in the process. The store was just an endless stretch of dry goods in boxes as big as my new safe.

After much side-tracking and lusting after various cereals, my last thought before dropping off for the night was *I should go to the grocery store tomorrow.*

Over the course of a week or so, I tried many configurations of tarps, tents, and two-by-fours in an attempt to make a good shelter.

Let me fucking tell you, you can never think of all the elements at once when you're building a new shelter. Tents are great for keeping out the rain, but if an animal or a person shows up, tents are not the most defensible things. In fact, you'd be just as well off in a wet paper bag. Also, if you use a flashlight inside a tent, you become a big fat visible glow worm in the night. No help for it.

If you use a candle, you also run the risk of turning your shelter into a melting aggregation of plastic, nylon, zippers, and death. The last problem was that there was still some small amount of ash falling from the sky, and when you unzip the side of a sloped tent in the morning, you dump all the ash that collected in the night right into your own face. Tents are not your friend.

After my experiments with tents, including making one out of heavy tarps with only slightly improved results, I thought I'd just take over someone's house. The question of the homeowners coming back did cross my mind, but would just have to hope that they understood. All the same, I tried to pick a house that looked like friendly people lived there.

Hateful hand-painted political signs on the lawn were discouraging. The same was true for 'security system' signs: The power may be out, but I knew that some of those sneaky fuckers ran on batteries in case some potential thief or ax murderer was smart enough to cut the main power first. How long do those batteries last? I didn't know. I wasn't even sure if having battery-backup was a common thing or reserved only for the super-rich and maniacally paranoid. I did know that they were made, though, and that meant somebody somewhere bought them. With my luck, the tiny "Protected by LockLand Security" sign would mean tripping a battery-powered banshee, broadcasting my location for a mile in this newly still city and drawing some psycho killer all the way from Lloyd District.

I also avoided houses with signs of children. Not only was I afraid of a protective momma and poppa bear coming back with big guns to find me in their house, but I was also afraid of what I mind find inside if the family came to grief before they could evacuate. Some things you just don't want to see. I could imagine at least a hundred of them.

More encouraging were houses painted bright, artsy colors. I assumed that the people who lived in these were a more peaceful and communal breed, who would gently put me out like a lovable rascal stray if they returned. There are plenty of cute little federal-style constructions in residential Portland, painted fabulous purple or pastel rainbow. I chose a bright blue one-story with rabbit sculptures on the overgrown lawn. It looked friendly. I smashed the smallest window I could and crawled inside: Mab, Queen of the Broken Glass.

Though I have more positive things to say about abandoned houses than I do about tents, in the end it was still no good.

First of all, once I was back under a roof, the fear of it falling down on me returned full-force. Watching my apartment collapse into the street apparently had some permanent psychological effects regarding my perception of stability.

Second, I'd just broken a window and had no way to seal it back up. Third, however much trash I hauled out into the back yard, the biodegrading smells of organic matter left behind had taken root in every porous surface in the house. Someone had spilled sugary liquid on the couch before leaving, and now it was molding. The compost was overgrowing its little tan bin. Given another week, the coffee grounds would probably eat through the plastic. All said, living in a house that made me want to vomit was not advisable.

Lastly, I realized that there were no longer really any advantages to living in a house. There was no water, power, or trash pick-up. Nothing I stored there would be any safer than it was in the park, because even if I had the keys to the locks, someone else would take out a window just like I did. The only consolation offered by living in this wooden hulk was that it was camouflaged shelter: One house in a block, a neighborhood, a city, not that different from any other when it came to attracting looters or crazy survivalist gangs. I thought about all of this while I explored its dark, lifeless rooms.

When I got back to the living room, another small earthquake hit. The picture window shattered when the wrought-iron lamp fell into it. I leaped through that gap like a circus tiger. It wasn't until the panic subsided, and my pulse stopped hammering in my neck, that I realized I was bleeding all over the place. I was going to die.

Of course, once I found the measly little nick on my hand, I knew it wasn't going to kill me. It was my own fault, really. I tried to return to civilization after it had clearly kicked me out, and it bit me. I wouldn't make that mistake again.

The last unsuccessful thing I tried was to use the playground in the park as the basis for a fort. There was a sort of shelter there, little boxes and metal cages connected by rope bridges and plastic slides. These things were designed to take the kind of abuse doled out by eight-year-olds, but not designed for earthquakes. As soon as I stepped on the ladder of four-by-fours, the whole thing fell down.

And this is why, the night before the Great Grocery Adventure, I wrapped my moped in a dark green tarp and crawled into a new kind of shelter. I'd found a mostly-metal desk left out at the sidewalk with a 'free' sign on it, possibly fated for a trash pick-up that never came. Two sheets of plywood from a construction site made wind-proof walls. With a brown tarp and some branches over the whole thing, it was effectively the coziest hunting blind that ever was.

I didn't even care that my feet stuck out.

The morning of the Great Grocery Adventure, I crawled out of my shelter to find that the ash fall had doubled in intensity. Clouds were piling up in the sky. It wasn't raining yet, but thunder to the west hinted that it was a coming attraction. At first, I thought my sense of direction had skewed about ninety degrees because the sun appeared to be rising in the north.

I squinted at the red glow on the horizon. Couldn't be sunrise. In Portland, there's usually enough cloud cover that it takes three hours to be sure the sun came up at all. That would definitely have been the case today. Suddenly I found myself longing for the days when persistent rain was my number one complaint, because I'd realized why the sun was rising in the north. It wasn't the sun.

It was Mount Saint Helens.

The volcano was pitching the biggest hissy-fit of all time. I should never have been able to see it from Portland, but the volcano had been building on itself. I could see it glowing through the pines and firs of the park and fifty miles of ash-filled sky.

That was the day that many existing mountains in the Cascades, and some new ones, went the geological equivalent of nova. After crouching, quivering, and staring for a while, I came to the conclusion that this was the predicted event that triggered the evacuation of not just Portland but a large portion of the west coast.

I crawled back under my desk like a Cold War era schoolchild during a bombing drill.

The Mount Saint Helens eruption in the 1980's was more than a thousand times the force of the Hiroshima bomb. Now, not only was that repeating itself, but it was echoed up and down the Cascade mountain range as if Saint Helens had walked between two mirrors.

Looking at the glowing sky up and down my part of the planet was enough to tell me what was happening. All I could do was hide. I went back to my desk, turned on one of the light-up dog collars, and tried to read the paperback from my purse while the mountains roared. Some part of me was waiting for the lava, but it never came. Instead, it started pouring outside. Ash-water came into my shelter. Time to move.

I spent a very muddy, hyperventilating half-hour digging out my food-safe and relocating the stash to my backpack and the storage compartments on my moped. The wetter my white scarf got, the worse it served as a dust mask, but I kept it on because it had become kind of a security blanket for my face. The whole world dripped with grey slurry. I imagined that I looked like a swamp monster.

When there is enough time, a person can experience a kind of low-grade panic that lasts for hours but never peaks, never takes over. While packing up as best I could, I was experiencing a transition from that kind of panic to what most people probably think of as the 'real' kind. The kind that makes your guts want to turn inside out, makes your eyes water, splits your mind into every possible faction and then sets them on each other in a cerebral bar brawl. Things were starting to get rough and sparky in the Synapse Saloon.

Stay in the park! Plants absorb water!

Get out of the park! I don't give a fuck what you say about plants, it is clearly flooding!

SO IS EVERYWHERE ELSE!

Run! Get on the moped and RUN!

You can't run the moped in this!

FOOL! IDIOT! BLITHERING IDIOT FOOL! You have to get out of here!

You'll kill yourself if you try to drive in this! Even if you don't, you'll choke the engine!

BAD! BAD THINGS ARE FALLING FROM THE SKY!

You're no help at all, Crazy Mab. Get back in your box.

Eventually, the water started winning out over the ash. Afternoon saw me walking the still-tarped moped down Fremont Street, kicking floating branches, trash bins, and the occasional dead bird out of my way. Ash was clearing. Living birds were flying. Water was draining. I still had most of my stuff. The desk-shelter might even be there when I went back. Panic was subsiding. Possibly there could have been better outcomes to the first bombastic ash storm After the Suck, but I couldn't think of any. I was off on the Great Grocery Adventure, halfway to Eighty-Second Avenue. To my credit, I had only dropped the moped and fallen on my ass twice.

At the intersection of Fremont and Sandy, I ran into a problem.

There was a long-standing construction zone at these relatively major cross-streets. Counting the residential side streets, it was a kind of sloppy six-way intersection, a place where drivers constantly fear being pulled over for doing the wrong thing and no one ever wants to make a left turn. There was always at least one lane and two sidewalks under construction at any given time, though any work crew visible at the site always seemed to be rolling their eyes and doing not much, as fed up with Fremont and Sandy as everyone else. This intersection had wreaked havoc for years, and now, it seemed, it had had its havoc wreaked. Trees from the median on Seventy-Second had been uprooted and washed up against dump trucks. Vehicles of all kinds were sliding on the grey mud into a massive pile, forming a barricade at the southwest corner of the intersection. It was still moving, inch by grinding inch, down the hill, pushing safety cones and downed traffic lights in its path.

But the lumbering traffic plug wasn't the problem. The problem was the lack of Seventy-Second Avenue. Specifically the entire northbound lane.

I considered trying to make a fifteen-foot jump on a moped. Obviously, it wasn't a good answer, but my panic level was still at a good five out of ten, and when that's the case, the body will start to act on the first idea it gets before fact-checking it for contents of sanity or reason. It was fortunate that I only got to 'looking around for a ramp' before the sudden-death buzzer in my brain went off. Bad idea. Bad.

Most of the ideas that followed, as I walked in search of a way around the chasm, were just as bad or worse. I *could find a working truck, drive it into the hole, and use it as a bridge*. This would have sucked for two reasons: One, the hole was a lot deeper than your average truck was tall, and two, it would mean being *in the truck* when it suddenly dropped twenty feet, face first.

I got all the way down to Sacramento Street before the gap widened enough to eat the houses on either side. I could see that it got wider and deeper as it passed through a golf course where Seventy-Second stopped. I turned back.

Going north instead, I encountered a similar view. Northeast Going Street was going, going, gone. I toed the edge and looked down. There was a segment of burst pipe down there, oozing something unspeakable. Past the lip on the other side, it looked very much like the golf course. Same shit, different direction. On my way back to Fremont and Sandy, I kicked a floating bottle and it shattered. Mab, glass-killer extraordinaire, needed a plan again.

The next one I came up with was, in fact, a bad plan. I did it anyway.

Picture once again poor little Mab, all by herself. She's hidden her moped, backpack, and umbrella behind a house, to keep them safe from any big scary raiding parties. All of her stolen dog leashes have been tied together with the only good knot she knows. She's managed to climb up a miraculously standing telephone pole and tie the leashes around it, just above where the streetlight attaches. It's getting dark out. She's wearing a light-up dog collar around her neck in addition to the spiked and utility ones on her hips. At the moment, it's been turned off to save the battery. The precious crowbar is tucked into her pants. She pulls the leashes as far out as they go and walks to the edge of the urban canyon. The hesitation is barely noticeable. She runs around the telephone pole in a huge circle, holding the taut leashes by the convenient loop. She gains speed. At the edge of the pit, she launches herself into the air: Jane of the Jungle, the Human Volleyball, Centrifugal Force Girl. For four seconds, she flies. And of those four seconds, she only screams in terror for three.

The fun way of looking at this new landscape was "The world is my obstacle course." I'd been forced to run the usual set of plastic dangers in elementary school, where they gave us five minutes to dodge cones, jump ropes, and climb the same pieces of playground equipment that we voluntarily faced every day, but I hadn't done anything like it since then. There were a few big differences between that and this new, adult version. For one, there were no instructions for how to run the course. It didn't even necessarily have all the equipment. For another, it left me with a consistent and nagging fear of the adult equivalent of the next skinned knee, because the 'skinned knee' of the grown-up Fun Run could be a broken leg, or a broken neck. Still, with each thing that I managed successfully, I found that I was a little less afraid and had a little more fun. The occasional screams started shifting in pitch and intensity. At this point, they were still somewhere between "Falling Down Stairs" and "Bungee Jumping." At least they'd lost the overtones of "Being Ax-Murdered."

Before I even got to Eighty-Second Avenue, I found another sudden drop off. This time, it wasn't just a crack in the ground, unless you can count several square miles as one big crack. I wondered if the outlying regions had dropped thirty feet, or if most of Northeast Portland has just risen out of the rest of the ground.

Rather than an incisive border between the two areas, there was a nice slope made by a small landslide. It wasn't all nice . . . in some places, it was a house-slide or a school-slide, but it was hard to feel bad for the empty buildings even if they were beloved by somebody somewhere. The people who lived in those houses weren't here. I was. And for me, this lovable little landslide meant a smooth trip down what would otherwise have been a really nasty hill. I scouted around for a sled.

Fifteen minutes later, I was bombing down the new muddy hill on a car hood I found leaning against the wall in a body shop. The hood ornament had crunched into the slag and broken off as soon as I hit my new sled, which I did in a flying leap, making a sound that hardly resembled an ax-murder-victim scream at all. Echoing around in the ash-coated dusk, it sounded a lot more like . . .

"Woo-WHOOOOOOOOOOOOOOYEAAAH!"

It was smooth sailing down Eighty-Second Avenue for quite some time, alternately carrying the car hood over my head as a shield and using it as a toboggan on any downhill slopes. I caught a huge break when it came to post-apocalyptic travel. Even though the hood was heavy, and the walk was long, it was practically a vacation. I found a vet's office, and when I broke in, there was not only good stuff like clearly labeled antibiotics and pain medications but also a candy jar on the counter. I sat at the corner of Northeast Schuyler and ate the entire half-pound of caramels. From there, I could see my next obstacle. The Highway Eighty-Four Overpass had become the Highway Eighty-Four Fuck-all. Smooth pavement gave way to chaotic rubble, and somewhere down there, something was smoking. I would have to take a detour.

A detour was fine by me, because the bulk foods store I planned on hitting up was a few blocks east anyway. I jumped a fence and moseyed across the vacant Eighty-four. No matter how empty the world is, or for how long, there is still a little alarm that goes off in a girl's head when she walks down the off-ramp of a major highway. It says, *You are going to get hit by a car.* Eventually, though, when the mixture of desperation for company and survival cockiness brews up to a nice foam, the response to that alarm is, *Meh.* Big deal. Bring on the cars.

I weaved through the residential area on my way to One-Hundred and Second. It was farther than I'd remembered. Of course, when consistently traveling by moped, or any vehicle that requires no effort from the rider to make it go, distances get warped very easily. Once upon a time, in my brief car-owning days, I'd driven from New York to California in less than a week. The same trip on foot might take a year. Or the rest of my life. Also, passing by the Great Lakes probably wouldn't be so pretty now that they were one giant bathtub of floating death.

But anyway. I was talking about food.

The WinCo on One-Hundred and Second was built like a gigantic toad: Low to the ground, neutral in color, and in some oblique way, radiating grumpiness. As I skulked across the white-striped crosswalk to the doors, I tried not to think *Frog tongue.*

Someone had been here before me. The doors were smashed, and most of the glass had been swept aside. I figured that was all right. It would take ten people ten days to clean this place out. Hell, even if they were still in there, we would probably never be able to find each other if we were trying. I turned my dog-collar light on and held it out in front of me.

Damn, was it dark in there.

When good things happen to a person, the correct response depends on what he or she believes. Some fall on their knees and thank a god or goddess. Some give a big hats-off to the ancestral spirits. If you're more of an atheist gambling type, it's okay to thank the Lady as long as you don't name her. If you're an atheist who doesn't believe in luck, I'm not sure what you're supposed to do. Thank Neil DeGrasse Tyson next time you see him, maybe.

Finding a cleverly-placed rack of fireman's flashlights right inside the door, still half full, made me try to do all of those things at once. From the outside, it probably looked a lot like me doing a bad victory dance and making a quiet but extremely pleased "Nyuh!" noise. Flashlights! All mine! Of course, I couldn't carry twenty or thirty of them, but I obsessively unwrapped them until I realized that I had far surpassed my carrying limit. One in the hand, two in the pockets, two in the ever-present and thoroughly bulging purse.

I don't know if anyone else remembers these handy flashlights from the Y2K scare, but I thought they were the coolest toy ever when I was little. They're just one piece, with nothing to unscrew or replace. The on/off switch glows in the dark. I remembered them.

My mom used to take the Y2K flashlights away from me on the rare occasion that the power went out, because they only lasted for about eight hours. I killed them quickly. I just ran around waving them in rooms that were already perfectly well-lit with candles and camping lanterns. They made a sort of three-panel beam on the ceiling. I angled them back and forth, highlighting three chairs, or lining up the three points of brightest light across the surface of a window. My mother came up behind me and plucked the magic piece of plastic out of my hand. "I know you're having fun, but we have to save these," she said. "We might need them later."

I needed them now.

Playing with my new black-and-orange version, I realized that the one I had just picked off the rack didn't give the same kind of light. It was whiter, more even. In order to find out why, I looked directly into the flashlight and blinded myself.

Minutes later, a less stupid investigation proved the new flashlights to be LEDs. Civilized man had said goodbye to the old-school light bulbs some time in the last ten years or so. This one would last a hell of a lot longer than eight hours. I wanted to run back to my childhood and kiss Bill Nye the Science Guy on the cheek. The advance of technology had been productive! Yes, Virginia, there IS a silicon! I shined the flashlight on its own package. 150+ hours of light. These things were my new best friends. I fit another one in my pocket and stuffed one in each cup of my bra. These flashlights and I were intimate now, and we were never going to be apart again.

I tried various shopping carts until I found one that didn't squeak like a cat toy. Creeping between the towering stacks, I ducked my head but I wasn't at all sure why.

What would be the best stuff? I knew what I wanted. I wanted twenty fast-food cheeseburgers, a gallon of fresh banana smoothies to wash them down with, and a kiddie pool full of Ben & Jerry's Pistachio Pistachio for dessert. Since there was probably no more ice cream south of Alaska and wild bananas weren't common in Oregon, I grudgingly filled my cart with less perishable stuff.

Pasta. Peanut butter. Off-brand toaster pastries in a box so big you could use it to move. Soup. Cheese puffs in a plastic barrel. Tuna. Water. Flavored water. Vitamin water.

Water is heavy. It's the worst thing to go without, and the worst thing to carry. I loaded up and tried not to think about how I would deal with it later.

When I got to the rows of bulk dispensers, I opened up a plastic bin full of pretzels and sat down, eating handfuls, spraying salt all over the concrete floor. They were stale. It didn't matter. I realized how chapped my lips were when they started to sting from the salt. The vitamin water intensified it. Pain was becoming more urgent than hunger.

I got up and started shuffling around, holding my

mouth, looking for a giant pack of Chapstick. I found small tubs of store-brand petroleum jelly instead. That stung worse.

My life over the next half-hour was mostly about trying to ignore the suffering my face insisted on doing.

Pre-Suck, there had been many times when I'd successfully dealt with annoying pain in a mind-over-matter way. Eyebrow plucking. Flu shots. Bikini waxing. Stupid household injuries. And now it's time for another edition of my favorite segment, "Let me fucking tell you."

Let me fucking tell you, it's a hell of a lot easier to concentrate on overcoming pain in a doctor's office, or the safety of your own bathroom when you have nothing else to do except heal and maybe shower, than it is while you're trying to sort through expiration dates on packages the size of washing machines in a dark store the size of two football fields.

In the middle of this attempt to multitask, I heard a noise.

Scrabbling on the concrete floor.
A loud bang.
Scrabble.
Clank.
Screaming.

Once again, I thought *this is it. I'm going to die.* I was going to die in WinCo with petroleum jelly on my face and pretzel salt on my shirt, covered in ash and dressed like a rejected character concept from a post-apocalypse video game. So much for going out young and pretty.

With an unusual amount of foresight, I waited until there was another loud noise to click off my flashlight. It was the only noise I made for ten minutes. The screaming had stopped, but a chuffing noise had replaced it, and the scrabbling and clanking sounds continued. It was coming from the giant section of meat coolers in the back.

I couldn't run from this store. I needed it. I needed five pounds of off-brand toaster pastries like I'd never needed anything before in my life. Slow as stop-motion, I got my knife out of my purse and minced my way down the toiletries aisle toward the sound.

I waited at the end.

The noises had stopped.

I couldn't move for what seemed like forever, and must have been at least five minutes.

Then I turned on my flashlight.

Here's something to remember about trying to decide whether or not you're in mortal danger based purely on auditory input: Raccoons can make a noise that sounds very much like a human screaming.

Something else to remember is that, when it comes to waiting out an anomalous noise, just about everything in nature is more patient than humans.

Momentarily trapped in my flashlight beam was a coyote. It was staring at me, standing on top of a cooler full of rancid meat, a dead raccoon hanging in its jaws.

Before I had time to process what I was seeing, I panicked at having seen a pair of eyes staring back at me. I shut the flashlight off and threw myself back behind some giant packages of toilet paper, trying to remember how to deliberately execute the bodily function 'breathing' instead of 'pissing oneself in abject terror.'

The coyote fled in the dark. Canid toenails clicking on a floor used to be a noise that meant a dog was coming to annoy you while you were trying to sleep. Now, the long-buried monkey brain conclusion resurfaced: The click of Canid toenails mean that something is coming to shred you into little tiny pieces and eat you.

If not for the recent injection of water and salt into my system, I would have passed out right then. The floor was cold, but I was covered in a gross sweat. I couldn't open my eyes because they were full of volcanic ash mud. I may have been crying. I don't really remember. The concrete floor was cold, so I laid down on it. An hour must have passed before I recovered enough to get up and go about my grocery gathering. Even then, I was convinced that something bad had happened, even though I was physically unharmed and mostly functional. Obviously, the raccoon got the worst of the whole ordeal, not me. Still, I shook and panted and tried to stop my eyes from rolling back in my head while I made my way back to my shopping cart.

Fucking coyote!

By the time I left WinCo, I was loaded down with goodies and pushing a shopping cart to boot. I had found a little plastic cup full of carabiners at one of the check-outs and clipped reusable bags with the big recycling logo all over myself and my purse. Vienna sausages stacked high in plastic wrap leaned halfway out of the cart, jolly blue labels jiggling with every rotation of the cart wheels. Fifty feet of clothesline hung around my neck. I started to whistle before I realized that I'd salted my lips too badly to do so. Vitamin water sloshed in the rack under the cart. I was so overcome with joy at my acquisitions that I wasn't even distressed when I realized how heavy it all was. That was fine. Heavy was good.

It had stopped raining and mostly ceased to ash as well. I would just take my time getting back to my camp.

In the end, it took almost three days, but for those three days I had food, water, and light, so they were pretty much spent in paradise.

Most of that return trip requires no description. There were periodic stops for redistribution of weight, for waiting on labored breathing to slow, for nibbling on bits of my haul. Stopping for the night in vacant garages worked out well for me despite the hours spent lying awake, afraid the roof was going to fall in. I learned to live with some base level of fear. It wasn't so bad. Fear might eventually destroy my adrenal gland, but it was probably doing me a whole lot of favors in the meantime by keeping me from killing myself.

Getting my stash on wheels up the hill I had sledded down was hard. Getting it across the gap at Fremont and Sandy was harder. After much thought, I swung every individual bag and box across with me one at a time, using a downed sign post to tease the rope back to me after each release. There was probably a better way, but I'd thought of one that worked and couldn't really be bothered to come up with another. I couldn't swing the shopping cart with me, so I tried to throw it to the opposite side. Unsurprisingly, this didn't work at all. The cart ended up at the bottom of the giant crack in the street. I flexed my arms and realized they no longer contained even the pitiful amount of strength they'd had to start with. Time for a break.

I tried to eat some mixed nuts I'd bagged up, but my hands were too sore and weak to crack open the pistachios. I picked out all the cashews and sealed the bag back up.

I thought about how good it was that I'd realized about the boiled-noodle arms before I'd tried another swing across the gap.

There didn't seem to be any immediate danger, so I shuffled my remaining east-side food to safety and swung myself, with no additional weight, across by crook of my elbow to hide my west-side pile. Then I broke into a nearby drug store and took a nap in their only chair. It had a blood pressure cuff and some drug advertisement attached to it. It was quite comfortable.

Sleep lasted for an hour or two before worry chased it off. Even while it did last, I dreamed about empty cupboards and opening refrigerator doors to find black holes.

Once everything (except the cart, may it rest in peace) was on the west side of the canyon, I had to figure out how to carry it all at once. Notions of making multiple trips all the way to my camp and back were promptly smacked down with a mental baseball bat. The moped would only carry a fifth of the haul at a time, and some of the boxes were too big even to strap to it safely.

I spent about half an hour looking around for cars before realizing how lucky I would have to be to find a working car and matching keys.

The problematic bulk of my food was only slightly lessened as I sat in the street, munching strawberry toaster pastries, staring at the cornucopia of preservatives and wondering what to do.

Classes I Wish They Had Taught In School:

How to hot-wire a car
Types of knots and their uses
First Aid 202, or, What the hell is gatafloxacin?
How to predict weather by looking at the god

damn sky
How to identify edible wild things
How to identify toxic wild things
How to identify predatory wild things from at least a mile away
How to turn nature into yummy junk food
Cloth-making, carpentry, blacksmithing, hunting, fishing, meat-curing, water sanitation

Maybe just a course called "Post-Apocalypse Survival for Complete Idiots." We teach college courses in Vampire Literature but we don't teach people how to take care of themselves. I'm never going to understand that.

At the intersection of Fremont and Sandy is a store called Daddies Board Shop. One of the windows, fractured and sharp, was still partially held together by a Toy Machine sticker of a red devil-monster. I gingerly ducked under the monster three or four times on trips to get longboards before paranoia got to me and I smashed him with the crowbar, clearing out the windowpane entirely. Monsters. Just what I needed.

Once I had a good number of longboards in the street, I lashed them all together with grip tape to make a twenty-wheeled cart. Experimentation ensued, mostly in the form of kicking and dragging. My new improvised cart wiggled like crazy when it moved. I enhanced the stability by laying disassembled longboard decks across the existing platform and putting a few screws in each.

Better.

I've never really built anything more complicated than a birdhouse before, so what I can now identify as a novice's tendency to over-engineer reared its head and I started to wrap the whole thing in more grip tape. The tape ran out halfway through.

Good enough.

I hooked the whole thing up to my moped with some of the clothesline, strapped down the food, and puttered off towards Wilshire Park.

The longer I went without seeing fellow human beings, the less paranoid I was about harm coming to me from that quarter. I mean, zero out of every zero human beings is an ax murderer. Zero is actually a pretty good number. That night I put most of my wrapped-up food stash out of easy animal reach and left it at that.

While I'm on the subject, here's a tip from dinner that night: Don't drink the water. Drink the vitamin water, the bottled tea, or the non-caffeinated soda. I drank the water, but I also could have used it to cook with and rehydrate things like pasta.

Do not cook with vitamin water. Not even if you don't want to drink it because it is your least favorite flavor.

Do not cook with vitamin water *especially* if it is your least favorite flavor.

Mixed berry rotini is no good at all.

It occurred to me that night, after I'd crawled back under my desk and spent an hour reading my last paperback in the world (*Pattern Recognition* by William Gibson), that I was repeatedly missing some vital elements to survival. Food, water, and shelter were the immediate physical stuff, but unless I wanted to wander around losing my mind until I blew myself up trying to barbeque squirrel meat on a broken propane grill, there were a few other requirements. Knowledge. Information. Other people. Music. A change of clothes. Getting laid every once in a while. It may not be true for the less brain-heavy animals, but for modern humans, these are the things of which sanity is made. In the morning, I would try to find some of them. For now, I turned off my flashlight and stared at its little ribbed switch glowing in the dark. Most of my life, my way of going about things had been shaped by access to the internet. My cell phone was off and securely packed away, because the last time I'd tried to use it I hadn't had much luck. As a web-capable unlimited-calling piece of modern technology, it made a hell of a flashlight.

Libraries were still a thing, right? Maybe I would try to find a library. I put my fingers to my temples, trying to conjure an image of a library. Hidden in the depths of my brain were the images and locations of quite a few. Most of them were in New York. One of them was from a painting of the Library of Alexandria burning. Some conditioned section of my brain kept insisting that I should just look up libraries on Google Maps or Wikipedia. When I beat that suggestion down, another one popped up like an idiot whack-a-mole: *Well, then you should ask someone*!

Of course, there wasn't anyone to ask. If there was, I wouldn't be having this stupid conversation with the auto-thoughts in my head.

I would find a library. I would find information on how to survive this life After the Suck, and how I could find other people. Possibly I would learn homesteading skills like how to card, rhett, and weave, though I didn't know what two out of three of those even meant. They were done by a character in a book I read once. They might have something to do with sheep.

Maybe wherever the rest of humanity was, they had sheep. Goats, chickens, cows, dogs, cats . . . I hoped there was a farm somewhere with every animal in the children's books. Otherwise, mankind had wasted all those thousands of years on domestication and selective breeding, and that would just be a shame.

Maybe they had pigs. Maybe there would be bacon. I started to fall asleep imagining an idyllic, isolated ranch somewhere that had been totally untouched by the Suck. They would be surprised when I told them my horror story. They would mourn for all the lost people at first, but after a few months they would make awful jokes about how that's what Aunt Peggy got for moving away to the big city. They would have a smart cattle dog, a lovey-dovey cat, and horses who behaved like they understood every word you said. I would wear pants and swear like a ranch hand, but learn to help out in the kitchen, too. I would name a piglet in the spring and eat it when it was grown.

That's what my life had come to. My biggest fantasy involved giving an animal a name and then eating it.

I moved on to other thoughts. Would electricity ever come out of the walls again? Hot water? Internet?

There was a small earthquake that night, but I couldn't even be bothered to worry about it. I just fell asleep.

CHAPTER THREE
THE PLAN

There are, in fact, more than a dozen public libraries in Portland, Oregon. Some of them are big, obvious things with classy signs out front. I probably passed within a few blocks of some of these on my initial search. I made it all the way to Lloyd Center thinking of the giant bookstore there, but Lloyd Center is a mall that is mostly built on a combination of its hollow self and parking garages. Architects, planning the whole thing for Portland, hadn't exactly gone the extra mile to make it earthquake-proof.

Lloyd Center had not fared well. The little sky bridge between then main building and the parking lot across the street had snapped. The mall folded in the middle like the beginning of world's worst origami crane. The exploded contents of several stores lay in the street: Someone had pulled the little string on the mall and all the confetti popped out. Aeropostle and Hot Topic lay equalized on Halsey Street. Some contents of Barnes & Noble had made it out in a landslide. I picked up the first salvageable book I came to, just in case the universe had decided to throw me some kind of Deus Ex Machina bone. It was a copy of a teen vampire novel. So, too, were the second, third, and fourth books I picked up. I came to the conclusion that the universe did not like me much.

Leaving Lloyd Center behind, though, I started thinking about other book stores instead of libraries. There seemed to be three book stores for every commercial block in Portland. Not all of them would be helpful . . . some contained only feminist literature, discount textbooks, or various subculture manuals and 'zines. I knew where some of these were, and while *The Anarchist's Cookbook* may have been instructional in its own way, they did not, on the whole, contain the kind of broad-spectrum re-education I was looking for.

If only I could cross the river to get downtown! Powell's City of Books on West Burnside was the greatest collection of human thought and knowledge I'd ever seen. Pre-Suck (which I think from now on I'll just refer to as P.S.), I'd hardly ever gone there, because it was sooo far away, and books were sooo expensive. I could have handed over a little piece of plastic and walked away with instruction manuals for building a whole new god damn civilization. Puttering slowly up Martin Luther King Jr. Boulevard, I got down to the business of cursing my lack of foresight.

The ashfall had all but stopped, but the streets were still striped with sediment from the rain's attempt to wash away the volcano. Drainage had broken down entirely in some places. There were larger puddles than would be considered safe to drive through. Sometimes I had to take side-streets. Sometimes I just had to walk the moped through them.

I needed boots.

No. I wanted boots. I needed information.

It doesn't do to get sidetracked when you're on the

hunt.

Not even if your socks are squishy.

There was a building partially fallen into Martin Luther King Jr. Boulevard, so I took some side streets and ended up, after some weaving, on Knott Street.

There it was. The Title Wave.

The Title Wave is (based on information I found inside) the near-final resting place of retired library books from all over Multnohmah County. Libraries send them here and then, for some pocket change, people take them home forever. It looked like an old Spanish Mission to me, but my knowledge about architecture extends about as far as I can throw it. The architecture, that is, not the knowledge. And as far as feats of building-moving strength go, I'm not exactly making a career out of them. Actually, the building was still in good shape and even unlocked, but it still took me five or six tries to get the wooden double-doors open just because of their weight, so that probably tells you something.

Inside, there was still good light coming in through the windows. I only turned my flashlight on to read titles in the shadows of other shelves. No one was trapped inside. No one had raided it. The only sign of the earthquakes was some bookmarks that had fallen off the desk. It smelled like bookstores should smell. I seriously considered moving in.

I started a pile of books on the desk. Car maintenance. Well digging. Gardening. Geology of the Northwest. Geology in general. Maps. Cookbooks. Camping guides. Animal husbandry. Animal training. And from a funny little corner, tucked in among the science books, *Living off the Land* by Chris McNab.

Once upon a time, when there were post offices, a

guy in a blue uniform would come around and deliver a catalog called "Things you never knew existed and can't live without," or something like that. It was full of oversized shirts that said "Pour me another, you're still ugly" and resin-cast pocket watches with skulls and crossbones. These were neat. Looking at them entertained me, even if sometimes the joke shirts were so bad that I just raised an eyebrow trying to imagine the person who would wear them. They did not, however, belong to either category implied by the name on the glossy front. I was aware of the existence of bad joke shirts, and I could, in fact, live without personally owning a wide selection of badly-made plaster gargoyles.

But this book. *Living off the Land.* It really should have been called *Things You Never Knew Existed and Can't Live Without, You Spoiled Urban Brat.* I plonked down on a stepladder and read the first real chapter, and in that chapter I learned about "Rabbit Starvation," scurvy, and water purification. I learned that the things chick magazines had told me my whole life to avoid were things that I was literally going to die if I didn't eat. The book said, phrased in a very gentle way, that though few people would ever find themselves in survival situations, we should all have a basic knowledge of how to keep ourselves alive should the need arise. I closed the book. My interior monologue rephrased this message as *"You should have learned this stuff years ago, dumbass. It IS on the final exam."*

I opened the book again, set myself up a nest behind the counter, and fell asleep reading.

The next earthquake woke me up around three in the morning. It wasn't so much the shaking building that roused me, but the pile of books that fell off the counter and onto my legs. Suddenly my roof phobia was back full-force. I had to get out of there. I was going to get crushed. I needed to leave now. Now. NOW. I flailed around, trying desperately to get up.

The earthquake stopped. *Ground to a halt*, I thought, snorting. I hated puns and yet my brain insisted on producing them. It was bad, but not as bad as, say, the ceiling coming down on me.

Still. Three in the morning, alone, in the dark, after what was probably the end of the world. It's not a nice way to wake up.

By the time the sun started coming up, I had collected all the things I wanted from Title Wave and headed back to my little camp.

Along with a large number of books, I'd taken a few tee shirts off the shelf. They were promotional shirts for both the store and reading in general. I took a bunch because I vaguely knew I might need them for bandages or rope or something, but to tell you the truth, I wouldn't have minded wearing them, either. The shirts were right. Reading is god damn important.

Looking at the dash on my moped, I realized that there was one more book I really wish I had found: Siphoning Gasoline for Dummies.

Mopeds can run a long, long time on a liter of gas. The trouble is, there's a pretty limited number of liters per tank, and I was definitely into my last one. The needle in the scratched pane on my little rounded dash was wobbling around in an area I did not like one bit. Finding an open gas station wasn't likely. A few of the ones I had passed had signs saying they were out of gas. Sometimes the prices had been taken down, presumably because they were jacking up the cost per gallon as people filled up their tanks for the unexpected evacuation road trip. I remembered hearing somewhere that newer cars were almost impossible to siphon gas out of because there was some kind of new safety bit built in. Even if I could find a car, it might be made so that even people who knew how still couldn't siphon gas out of them. I didn't stand a chance. In the movies, people lift the covers off of the big underground tanks at gas stations and somehow get fuel out of them. Next time I passed a gas station, I pulled over and stared critically at the huge metal cover. I poked it with my crowbar. A conclusion was reached almost immediately. *Nope. Not happening. Thanks for nothing, writers of "The Walking Dead."* I poked around in the trashed gas station and scored some candy and some more Misty menthols. Figuring that sitting around doing nothing had given me most of my good ideas so far, I sat on the counter, swinging my legs, eating a Kit-Kat and smoking a cigarette, until something came to me. My muddy shoes shed flakes of ash on the floor with each kick. The silent store filled with wisps of smoke. While I considered things, I stole all their plastic bags and pocketed the few remaining lighters with decent designs on them. Anything with a bad cartoon skull got left in the rack.

Swing legs. Smoke cigarette. Stuff face with chocolate. Think.

At first, I made a mistake. I was thinking big. Underground tanks. Fuel stores for generators. Tanker trucks conveniently left on I-5. Even if I found these things, I wouldn't know what the hell to do with them. They were out of my power. So what was within my power?

Encouraged by the nicotine and sugar, the little Crazy Mab voice that lived in the attic over the rest of my brain started pitching in again.

Pshaaw. You're fine. You've got power over, like, mopeds and lawnmowers and little shit like that. What more do you need? Heehee.

Lawn mowers.

Thank you, Crazy Mab. You've been a great help.

Lawn mowers.

I grabbed some of the one-gallon emergency gas containers from under the counter and headed to the nearest residential neighborhood with big, grassy lawns.

Breaking into a garage with a crowbar is easy.

Finding someone in Northeast Portland who mows their own lawn is not.

I had made a bad assumption: People with big lawns will have big lawnmowers. It's just not true. People with big lawns have big budgets, and they hire someone else to mow their lawns.

Five garages later, I'd started to figure this out. Once I got to the outskirts of a nice neighborhood, I found a smaller house with a sign outside. A name. A phone number. The word "Landscaping." That was all the incentive I needed to break into their shed, which turned out to be a treasure trove of greasy equipment and small gas tanks, and in which I promptly started doing a dance of joy.

This dance of joy bears no resemblance to any civilized school of dance. It goes like this: Hold your arms out in the direction of the joyful thing like it's your long-lost puppy. Jump up and down while holding your arms out. Make a "Squeeee!" noise. Wiggle your upper body side to side while trying to use all the muscles in your face at the same time to grin like the biggest idiot you can. While doing all of these things, start spinning around in bouncy circles because one position cannot contain your joy. Once you're good and dizzy, go and embrace said joyful thing.

If it is a lawnmower, take this last step with caution.

Now, left to my own devices, I probably would have done a bunch of stupid shit like trying to tip the lawnmower over a bucket to get the gas out. Fortunately, I had someone else's devices. The shed was full of tubes, funnels, rags, and buckets. To my surprise, they were organized and in some cases even labeled, hanging on hooks or stacked in boxes. I always pictured people's sheds as more of a useful trash pile held together with motor oil and duct tape.

There was, in fact, duct tape. I put the roll around my wrist before I could forget about it.

I brought in one of the little red containers from my moped and set about learning how to siphon gas. Let me fucking tell you: Gasoline is one of the least pleasant things you might ever taste. It's not really good for chapped lips, either.

There are certain things a person should always take with them from a well-stocked collection of tools. If you should come across such a place, you want to pack up the duct tape, the WD-40, a good pair of channel locks, a small saw, safety glasses, and the best wrapping for all of these things that you can find. I really wish I'd known that at the time. I didn't. So I walked out of there with the duct tape, about three gallons of gas, and a length of hose . . . leaving most of the good stuff behind, feeling like a total success.

Back at my camp, I decided it was time to clean up a little. I shook the dried ash off of my desk-tarp in clumps and brushed off whatever still stuck. I climbed my food tree and double bagged everything, using the gas station bags and adding the new goodies to a branch and bag of their own. Kit-Kats deserved triple bagging. The best of the semi-perishables went in the buried safe after I gave it a good cleaning and drying. Books came out of the moped storage compartments and went into a salvaged milk crate that had once contained a sidewalk free pile.

I organized my bottled water by type. The moped received a good wiping-down with a book store tee shirt before being covered with the tarp for the night. I borrowed a broom from someone's front porch near the park and swept up around my camp. Just because it's the apocalypse, that's no excuse for getting sloppy.

Besides, the whole thing was a kind of meditation, and the result was a totally nonsensical peace: Everything is right with the world, because my moped is clean and my backpack is organized. Sometimes good things are stupid. I think that's okay.

There was a swing set still standing in the park. I took some of my new books over to it, so I could swing and read. Mostly, I just sat there and kicked my feet. It got dark. I took the books back to my desk and lay down under it with a flashlight to keep learning.

Some of the things I learned that night did not surprise me. Animal husbandry is largely really disgusting, having to do with reaching into parts of livestock that no sane human wants anything to do with and then, later in life, skinning and eating them. Dog training is a little like dealing with reasonably smart child who, nonetheless, doesn't really speak English. Well-digging is more complicated than it seems, the book on well-digging has a glossary for a damn good reason, and even with that glossary it was not something I was ever going to successfully engage in. When trying to garden, start with a reasonably well-stocked garden center to shop at. Working on cars is not so much a single activity one engages in as an entire science and art simultaneously, and I'm not sure how cars ever came to exist at all. With more study, I could probably glean more useful information from these books, but my first read-through offered the occasional factual tidbit buried in a whole lot of affirmation that I knew nothing about anything.

Then I got to the geology books, which gave me a surprising new perspective that I'd never taken away from my high school class on the subject.

I knew nothing about anything about geology. *And neither did anyone else.*

People are small. Our perception is limited. We build little tiny machines to try and see the bigger picture, and then other machines to interpret what the first machine is trying to tell us. This may have gotten us a long way from "The Earth is flat," and "Stars are holes in the sky-blanket," but compared to the omniscient gods we think we are, we just do not know shit.

The geology books were full of events that we couldn't predict and predictions that hadn't come to be. The only accurate predictions had been made weeks or even days before the event, which, in geology time, is like the millisecond between a bullet touching a forehead and death. Not enough time to do a damn thing. Not even enough time to know what's happened. We had made a lot of educated guesses about the giant, giant planet over the years, and that was the best we could do.

Looking over some world maps meant to depict various qualities of the Earth, I did it, too. There was a big area in North America called the Canadian Shield. It was supposed to be the most geologically stable ground anywhere on the continent, a place of exposed

Precambrian rock that had shrugged off some glaciers in the last ice age and kept right on sleeping.

I couldn't stay in Portland forever. It had been weeks since I discovered that everyone else was gone, and people did not seem to be flooding back on the I-5. Not that they could, with Mount Saint Helens. Not from the north, anyway. Not that it mattered, because the whole damn city was shaking itself apart a little at a time. I could only kid myself about that for so long. I needed to start packing and go somewhere stable, somewhere that might even have other people. Maybe, in my fondest wishes, even electricity.

I had subconsciously been waiting around for a handy What-To-Do-Now flier to fall from the sky, and it wasn't working. In some disasters, there might have been a second sweep by the National Guard, or Japanese planes dropping aid boxes with parachutes full of ramen noodles and peanut butter, but what happened had been global and it had been bad. There might not be enough humans or functioning technology left to get organized. I had to make a plan on my own. Heading for geologically stable ground was the only idea, and this book, this map of the Canadian Shield, was the only clue. Saskatchewan was looking good, apart from being more than a thousand miles away, with the terrain in between being in either questionable or straight-up killer condition.

Trying to sleep that night, I buried my face in my new pillow (a bookstore shirt stuffed with bookstore shirts) and thought about what the ground might look like between my desk-shelter and a potential new lakefront equivalent in Canada. I tried to sort out whether or not it was really the best thing to do. And then I followed the longest and finest tradition of my species: I made an educated guess.

CHAPTER FOUR
GEESE ARE SCARY, DOGS ARE STUPID, EVERYTHING IS EDIBLE

Come hell or high lava, I was not letting go of my food stash. At the thought of moving on without it, I found myself climbing my food tree and lovingly hugging a giant box of toaster pastries. These bits of sugar and salt were going to be a part of me if it was the last thing I did. If someone had come upon me in this state and tried to take them away, I would have killed that person with my bare hands.

It finally occurred to me, in that moment of crazy, that a real weapon might be something I needed to add to my collective possessions.

There were some other things I probably ought to track down as well, if I was preparing for a long journey to quite possibly nowhere. Maybe I should find a faithful dog companion, a big shepherd that would bring me game to eat and warn me of danger. Yeah. That sounded good. I should also track down some of the supplies recommended for an emergency kit by *Living off the Land,* like fishing gear and water purification tablets. I didn't know where a person would have gotten water purification tablets even P.S., but the book was starting to make me feel like I had some idea what I was doing as long as I followed it to the letter, which meant finding some of the damn things. Thoughts like *I'll probably just fall into a river and die anyway* were becoming less frequent, replaced by *Even if the food runs out, I could totally catch a fish* and similar ideas. The glory of having a Plan (with a capital P) was going to my head. World, look out. I had a Plan.

I spent most of one morning re-packing my gear to make the most space and the most sense. I let the air out of some pre-packaged foods in order to squish them down. The frame-pack, after some experimentation and coaxing, fit most things that weren't food and even a few munchies on top. It's amazing what you can pack when you don't have five changes of clothes. Unfortunately, even with this near-perfect system of organization, I still couldn't take everything with me on my moped. Even if I found a trailer that would take everything, my moped would pull it along at a maximum of five miles an hour. That was no way to travel to Canada.

I was going to have to steal a car. I still didn't have the first clue how to do that, but my brain was starting to adapt to the new rules of the world. The idea formed slowly over the course of the morning, the part of my thoughts that was always looking for a better way to do things turning the sediment from weeks of experience into a pearl of wisdom. Like the gas thing . . . but . . . the other way around.

When I needed gas, I wanted to go to the gas station because it was habit, but I couldn't get gas there because there wasn't any. Now I needed a car, and I was looking around the streets because that's where the cars live. Habit. By the time I finished organizing my stuff and sat down to eat a lunch of Vienna sausages, chips, and bottled tea, the idea was almost ready.

Cars don't come from driveways. Cars come from a store just like everything else. Dealerships would still be full of cars. It's not like there was a rush to buy new cars when people are being evacuated, and just like the bulk foods store, it would take the world's biggest raiding party to clear out all the dealerships in Portland.

I didn't even have to steal a car, really . . . I could just . . . kind of . . . buy a car. Without money.

I went motionless, my mouth still full of cheesy potato chips. I didn't want to scare the idea off, and it seemed tenuous. This new concept was a delicate intangible rabbit that might run at any moment before I ever got ahold of it.

When you buy a car, you sign a bunch of paperwork, give them some money, and they give you a key, right? It even has some gas in it, for test driving or whatever. I'd never done it, having bought my only car from a friend and never owned one since, but that was how I imagined it worked. So I could just go to a dealership, and since there was no one to ask for money, and no one to give a shit about the paperwork, I could just take a car for a test drive and never bring it back. No one would even care.

It was, indeed, a whole new world.

I needed to find a dealership, but that was okay. I had another good idea about that. *Two in a row,* I thought. *I must be getting better at this.* I was totally capable of thinking old-school. I didn't need the internet. I was going to break into a house and steal their phone book! Brilliant.

It was unfortunate that the first two houses I went into, closest to the park, were not capable of thinking old-school. Hunt though I may, there was no phone book anywhere. Must have gone straight into the recycling, which was exactly what I had done with my own big yellow hunk of advertising when it got dropped on my doorstep. The second house also contained several mice and a raccoon that I assume got in through the cat door. We're going to pretend, for the sake of my dignity, that the raccoon 'briefly startled' me, rather than scared me out of my fucking socks.

I went to a third house and broke in as delicately as I could. Then, as an afterthought, I banged on the side of the house with the crowbar for a while to scare off any creatures that might be inside. No small furry things came rocketing out the window, but there was a noise from behind the house: A dog barking. It was unexpected, but after a minute I decided it was totally welcome. Faithful canine companion, right? I went around back and let myself into the fenced yard, where I found a big black dog with Cheetos stuck to his face.

He was lying in a circle of knocked-over trash bins, thumping his club tail. Shredded paper and plastic blew all over the yard. His reaction to me was to get as low to the ground as possible and whine, crawling toward me a little before scuffing his feet around and getting halfway on his back. He was skinny. His eyes were gummy and gross. Otherwise, he looked all right.

There was a dog flap set into the back door. I assumed that he's eaten everything in the house and then started in on the trash. There was also what may have been part of a squirrel at the other end of the yard, but I didn't want to look any closer.

Before I could decide what to do, the dog solved it for me. He belly-crawled up and put his head on my foot, tail thumping around in the trash. He wiped some Cheetos dust off on my shoe, sneezed, looked up at me, and made a *whuff* noise. I understood him perfectly. *Everything has gone all wrong and you are the only person I have seen. Oh please oh save me oh please.* Whuff, indeed.

I sat down and held out my hand for him to sniff. He made a valiant effort, then sneezed all over it. I didn't even recoil. I just narrowed my eyes a little bit at the universe in general and started rubbing the snot off on the dog, which he seemed to enjoy. When I got up, he followed me. Rather than break anything I didn't have to, I just shoved my bag through the dog door and crawled in after it. The bag seemed to be getting lighter as time passed. Maybe it was easier to build up muscle than I thought.

Inside, it was clear that the dog either suffered from the worst case of separation anxiety ever, or had literally tried to eat every single thing in the house. The living room was carpeted with the couch. Cabinets in the kitchen bore the evidence of long days of a dog trying to figure out how doors work. In the end, they had all been nosed open and raided. A bag of dry dog food had been demolished. Cans were spread all over the kitchen, some covered in teethmarks. Poor dog . . . he knew that food came out of them, he just couldn't figure out the pull-tabs. I opened one and dumped it in his bowl. He completely forgot I existed for the next five minutes.

The dog had done the work of finding the phone book for me. It was in front of the sink, half eaten. Still, the ads in the back were reasonably intact, and I learned the locations of ten car dealers in less than a minute. A stupid P.S. habit-thought suggested I should call first to see if they were open. I put my hand over my eyes. Adjusting was a slow process.

The dog, having eaten the entire can of wet food, proceeded to throw it up again.

For anyone who has never had dogs, a dog throwing

up can be almost as funny as it is gross. He always looks like he's very surprised this is happening to him. Then he thinks 'Well, I can just undo that' and tries to re-eat whatever it was that made him throw up in the first place. I'm not sure how dogs have survived as a species. Canis Domesticus: Eating the bad food twice for thousands of years.

When he was done, I dragged him out of the room by the collar before he could try again and poured out a quarter can of food for him there. This went over much better. I poured a little water into a cereal bowl as well.

In a moment of inspiration, I tossed a small pot, a bowl, a fork, a knife, a spoon, and a cup into a canvas shopping bag. I may not need them for toaster pastries, but they were something a person should have. The survival book told me so. All that pasta was going to be hard to eat without anything to cook it in.

Also, while I hadn't had a pet in my whole adult life, I had some vague idea that there was supposed to be . . . dog stuff. A leash, food bowl, little doggie jacket. Possibly some kind of igloo-shaped kennel. I started hunting around for those things and quickly amassed a pile of dog-related junk bigger than my own collective possessions. This caused me to re-think. Was a dog-shaped sweater with a picture of a dog on it really necessary?

The P.S. Cultural Hangover lasted only a second. Hell no, it wasn't necessary! The dog is already wearing a fur coat! Not only did his ancestors roam the open tundra, but his grandparents were probably working duck hunters or sheep worriers or something! The dog would be just fine without an extra layer of synthetic fuzz. I started picking things back out of the pile and throwing them into the destroyed living room. Sweater. Dog bed. Three kinds of leashes. Pet shampoo.

When I threw the rain jacket through the door, the dog bounded after it, brought it back, dropped it in front of me, and proceeded to roll back and forth on it like it was the world's finest cow shit. I looked at him blankly for a minute before picking it up and putting it on him. If the neon plaid plastic dog jacket was coming with us, he was going to carry it himself.

I picked out the longest leash and snapped it on the dog's collar, which was an acrobatic feat considering how hard he insisted on leaning on the backs of my knees. I also got the first good look at his collar. His name was Vet. I wondered why.

At first, I thought maybe it was short for Veteran, like he was some kind of war hero dog, or maybe a retired police dog.

Later, I would decide that it was short for Veterinarian, and his human had named him thus because he had spent his little doggie life winning the award for Most Likely to Need Emergency Medical Care. He made a career out of joyfully trying to get to the canine afterlife. For a while, though, I was happy and optimistic about him. He would chase off bears, bring me food, and guide me to safety in storms, or something like that. That's what faithful canine companions are for.

Vet made one last heroic effort to eat the couch while I went over the whole place a final time.

As it turned out, there was also a cat in the house. She was laying in the very center of a queen-sized bed, fat, happy, and surrounded by mouse bones and feathers like the high priestess of a particularly bloody cult. Her entire reaction to my entrance consisted of blinking twice before going back to sleep. Obviously, she was doing just fine, and if she decided to move on there was always the dog door, so I left her alone. It's possible that she also scared me a little. No matter how small it is, an animal with blood in its teeth can make a person very uncomfortable.

When I got back to the living room, Vet was lying on his back with a mouth full of pillow stuffing. His tail thumped. His eyes rolled in his head, and he sneezed.

I let us out the front door, intending to take Vet back to my camp. For some reason, I thought about the cat, and locked the door behind me.

In the very short walk between his house and my camp, Vet tripped me once, went into barking hysterics three times, and peed on every object taller than six inches. I, on the other hand, was too focused on Vet to do much of anything else, even though I had to pee as well. Peeing in peace required taking the extra step of tying Vet to a tree so he wouldn't knock me over and cause me to piss on my own feet. While tied to a sturdy maple, he freaked out, whining and barking and jumping and making every effort to hang himself on a low branch. I didn't know what else to do with him. It wasn't like I could shut him under my desk until he calmed down.

I wanted to read a little of the car book before I set off to try getting one, so I opened up a can of sausages and threw them as far as I could, one at a time, all around the park. When I freed the dog, he went after them and I dug the book out of my moped compartment. Five minutes later, he was laying on my feet and burping, but at least I got a chance to read.

My entire P.S. knowledge of cars would have fit on one and a half Post-It notes. They were big metal things that go, and sometimes you have to take them to a shop, and the people at the shop do a thing. If I really stretched myself, I could probably bullshit about 'seasonal tires,' 'synthetic oil,' and 'wiper blade replacements' for another two Post-It notes or so, by virtue of being aware that these were things. Car-related things, even. Probably.

If it came down to it, I wasn't totally sure about most of the inner workings of my moped, either, but I figured it was a motor vehicle and maybe my limited experience in tightening parts or having someone replace them and then tell me about it might translate to cars and make their complex inner workings less mysterious.

Compared to the modern car, my moped has the technological complexity of a toy from a fast-food kid's meal. I thought I knew a lot more than I did. I thought cars were kind of like simple metal humans . . . you know, the hand bone's connected to the arm bone, the arm bone's connected to the . . . whatever.

What's inside a car is more like guts, where every part is made of a different material, has a different job, and in some inexplicable way is connected to two or three other guts, and all the guts are bolted to the skeleton, which only resembles a human insofar as if you put a bipedal skeletal system through a trash compactor and then threw the whole thing into a black hole, it might come out shaped like that. Parts that have names and important functions are invisible until you pry other things apart. There is such a thing as a CV boot joint. When the "Check Engine" light comes on (part of a handy digital system called OBDII that can't be fully understood without dual Master's degrees in Automotive Engineering and Computer Science), it could mean: A) The engine is about to explode, or B) Someone didn't tighten the gas cap properly. Automatic transmission in a vehicle is a mind-boggling piece of technology all on its own. Hell, *power windows* were a piece of mind-boggling technology all on their own.

On top of all of this, no two makes and models are even remotely the same.

In my brief stint as a car owner, I had a Mitsubishi Mirage. That poor car spent a lot of time in the shop. I did go with it, mostly because I had to pay for things and I never did figure out how to get it to go to the mechanic on its own. Most of the time spent 'working on my car' consisted of me doing homework while someone else worked on my car. The people in my mechanic shop were decent, and unusually personal, so they would take the time to show me what was wrong with my car and how they were going to fix it. Somewhere in this process, a lady who worked at my shop wiped a lot of dusty grease off her hands and showed me where my air filter was and how gross it had gotten. So when a friend said he was going to replace the air filter in his car and invited me to hang out with him while he did it, I agreed. Normally I would decline for fear of looking like an idiot, but I wasn't the least bit embarrassed because I thought I knew all about this kind of thing. Air filters. Of course. But he had a Honda.

His was in such a different location that at first I thought he must have no idea what he was doing. But he did. I was the clueless one. That was the day that I decided there was just no learning about cars. Leave it to the professionals, baby. I didn't pretend to know anything about neurosurgery, and the inner workings of cars were not so very different.

Now all the professionals had buggered off and evacuated, probably straight into a bigger disaster than the one they'd left behind. Their brains, so full of useful knowledge concerning catalytic converters and what makes air conditioning smell funky, might be melted into a grease stain by a volcano or rotting at the bottom of a giant hole in the ground. For all I knew, a crack had opened somewhere so deep that they might still be falling down it, taking their shiny and hard-won brains on a journey to the center of the Earth.

In short, no one was going to help me find, start, or fix a car, so I had to do my best and hope like hell that there were never any urgent repairs to make. I kept reading my new manual.

Vet scraped off his jacket against a tree and threw up on my shoes.

I made sure to leave for my car-hunting expedition with daylight left to spare. The place I'd picked was relatively nearby, and advertised 'the best prices on used cars' in the phone book, which seemed ideal, because not only was it a short trip, but great prices on used cars usually meant 'old shit for sale, made before the invention of car alarms.' Sometimes it also meant that the cars had been made before seat belts were legally mandatory, but that was okay. I just wanted to avoid any shiny new vehicles that needed battery-powered keys or had security systems that I would accidentally set off when I tried to start the damn things. So, to the used car lot I went.

I thought it would be okay to take the moped and still take Vet. After all, his top speed was probably the faster of the two. I looped his leash around my handlebar and headed out.

The roads were cleared quite a bit. The ash had stopped, and what hadn't washed away as mud during the rain was starting to blow away as dust. Nothing was quite the right color, but at least the feeling that an emergency was currently in progress was fading. Now there was a feeling that nothing was happening at all. The lack of tire tracks on the road was strangely numbing. Vet and I plodded on down Mason Street. I got my first ash-induced nosebleed. There would be plenty more, but I stopped noticing them after a while.

Along the way, we passed a house that had burned down. I turned to Vet, who was weaving along the street with his tongue hanging out, and said, "Guess someone left the gas on, huh?"

Talking to a dog was almost a relief. I had been talking to myself, inanimate objects, plants, and the universe at large, definitely taking on a shade of Crazy Lady Feeding Birds in the Park Syndrome. Talking to a dog was practically normal. People do it all the time.

Well, used to do it all the time, anyway.

Stealing a car was, once upon a time, one of the most scary and bad-ass things a person could do. Movies were made about it. If you stole a nice car, lots of cops came after you, like you'd murdered someone instead of taking some metal and plastic that, according to a piece of paper and the DMV, belonged to someone else. It was the most expensive thing a person might ever buy, second only to a house. Cars were serious business.

Getting your driver's license was equated with freedom and adulthood. Owning a car was a matter of status as well as function. Lots of people borrowed money and ended up paying more than their car was worth just to have one, which was just one of those stupid P.S. systems we never thought about twice. Finding a job when you didn't have a car was nearly impossible. When cars were popular, people expected you to be able to get across major metropolitan areas in less than twenty minutes. Some jobs were entirely centered on having a car, like pizza delivery and taxi driving. Cars were important, and stealing them was a big, hairy deal.

It took me a while to adjust to my new reality as it concerned things like 'shopping.' There were no more cashiers, no more cops, and no more jails. Real scarcity was beaten back by the dramatic population decrease, and artificial scarcity had gone the way of the buffalo, 911, Asimov's Laws, and my house.

Stealing a car when no one else is around is a hell of a lot easier. You walk into a dark office . . .

No, wait. I'm not there yet. I forgot to explain about the goat.

Before we made it to the car lot, Vet let out a great sickly baying howl-bark and took off into a backyard, pulling my moped over on its right side by the leash and dumping me into the street. I yelped, checked myself for injury, and gave the universe a quick thanks that I was riding a moped instead of a motorcycle, which would probably have crushed my leg. I struggled out of my backpack and chased after the dog.

I could hear him around the back of a house, accompanied by other sounds my brain just wouldn't identify. When I rounded the corner, words started clicking into place to label the sounds and smells I'd picked up from the street: Farm. Bleating. Agitated clucking, confused barking, and the smell of a very organic kind of yard.

Portland is a very green, sustainability-favoring city. Almost every house has a garden. Some people take it a step further and build chicken coops in their back yards, then spend their social life pawning fresh eggs off on friends because no one can possible eat that many. It isn't such a bad way to live. But I'll bet it's a lousy way to try to evacuate, and that might explain why the former occupants had just let their metro farm loose in the yard before booking it for wherever-the-hell. Chickens don't travel well. I speak from experience.

In the yard, Vet was down on his belly with his ass in the air, barking at a black-and-white goat. The goat was lying on its back with its legs pointing stiffly at the sky, but was very clearly alive by the blinking and the occasional bleating sound. A flock of chickens had taken pathetic semi-flight and were now weighing down the branches of a crab apple tree like the world's dumbest Christmas tree ornaments. I skidded to a stop in some cedar shavings. Was I really seeing this?

The goat wobbled upright, jumped sideways, and fell back over.

One of the chickens went "Bwauk."

Yes, I decided. *This is probably really happening.*

Vet looked at me, then back at the recovering goat, then at me again. He resumed barking.

Thanks to years of living on the internet, I knew what a fainting goat was, so that didn't alarm me as much as it might have. Fainting goats are a breed that, when startled, keel over like little furry ships running aground at Cape Fear and play dead for a minute. YouTube, may it rest in peace, was full of them. There is a good reason for this. Frankly, fainting goats are hilarious.

While I scooped up the end of Vet's leash and warily eyed the chickens, I wondered if you could milk a fainting goat. Goat's milk cheese was a thing, right? So it must be possible to milk a goat. I decided to come back for it once I had a car. Maybe there would be some eggs from the chickens, too.

I took Vet with me and tied him to the moped again, because it seemed safer than leaving him with the goat. The rest of the trip to the used car dealer was made at two or three miles an hour, so I could just put my feet down if he tugged on the leash again.

Okay, now I've made it to the bit where I steal a car. Here's how a person acquires a car in a post-collapse world.

Materials: Flashlight, crowbar, patience.

Step One: Break into the main office (crowbar) and hunt around in the dark for keys.

Step Two: Find a key hanging right behind the service counter and decide that THAT IS THE CAR that the universe wants you to have.

Step Three: Go outside and try sticking that key into various car doors until it works.

Much simpler than it used to be.

In this case, the universe wanted me to have a deep blue Subaru Forester made in the early 2000's, when the design was somewhere between the old-school wagons and the new universal SUV shape. As soon as I opened the door, Vet jumped into the driver's seat and would not be moved. I backed away from the car, and he followed me, but as soon as I went towards the car again he was right back in there, waiting to go for a ride while obstructing it from happening. Finally I just shoved him into the passenger seat. The next ten minutes were spent trying to re-familiarize myself with driving a car.

Much like repairing them, the actual experience of driving each make and model of car is different. Some have high beams that toggle on and off when you pull back on a lever. Some have emergency brakes where the center console should be. Some have all the dash instruments stuck in the middle of the damn car, instead of in front of the driver where they belong. You know, just in case your passenger wants to know what percentage of your oil life is left.

As I tried to fiddle with the headlights and nearly had a heart attack when the windshield wipers started going instead, I cursed car manufacturers all the way back to Henry Ford. It was like the standard-issue nightmare about forgetting how to walk. I couldn't drive a fucking car. Vet jumped into the back, not wanting any part in my cursing and experimentation. I didn't blame him.

Once I had things more or less figured out, I gave a sigh of relief for automatic transmissions and promptly ran into another car. But only a little.

After so long on a moped, driving a car was like wearing a fat suit. And not just wearing a fat suit. It was like wearing a fat suit on a very small off-Broadway stage, in a play about someone who collects china figurines.

I got out of the car, but I didn't check the damage. Looking at the headlight I busted was not going to do any good. Instead, I leaned my moped up against the Subaru and managed to push it up the side onto the roof. Bungee cords and towing straps abounded in the car lot, so I used as many as I could fit over the moped and through the windows to strap it down. Then Vet and I headed back to camp. I may only have been going ten miles an hour, but Vet thought it was the world's greatest thrill ride.

On the way back, I stopped for the goat. A chicken followed me to the car, so I took it with us in a little wire cage I found in the back yard. This was officially my weirdest road trip gang ever.

Back at camp, I drove the Subaru right across the grass and parked next to my desk. The entire afternoon was dedicated to filling the car up with food and hacking up some of the plywood to make a backseat barrier between Vet and the goat. While I worked on that, kicking and hacking and pulling and bouncing up and down and yelling, the dog and the goat stared at each other suspiciously. Sometimes Vet would bark, and the goat would faint. Then Vet would go over, sniff it, and retreat at great speed as soon as the goat made a noise. I probably would have laughed if I weren't so busy trying to cut one stupid piece of wood in half.

Indignity started building pretty quickly. I can survive the end of the world, swing over an asphalt-lined pit on a string of dog leashes, and steal a car, but I can't cut a piece of wood the shape I want? Ridiculous.

Through trial and error, I learned about wood grain. Once I figured out that I was trying to cut something against the grain, using a pretty lame selection of tools, I had a moment of clarity as to why I was just shredding plywood into splinters. A further few minutes of experimentation gave me an idea. I tossed the first of my former desk walls and grabbed the other one.

I don't recommend the following for any nice, finished-looking construction, but for cutting a board in half against the grain, this works: Score both sides with a giant kitchen knife. Then run over it with a moped. It will crack in half nicely, and can then be used to separate a big dumb dog and a fainting goat in the back seat of a Subaru. Or, you know, whatever you were going to use it for.

I used the other half of the board to cover the food in the very back of the car. Not only would it serve the purpose of keeping Vet out of my toaster pastries, but it also made it look like I didn't have any food in case any roving looters found the car and took a gander inside. It seemed like the less I saw of people, the more paranoid I was that they were out there and they were going to get me. In my mind, 'other humans' had gone from probable friendly rescuers to terrifying survivalist ninjas out to eliminate any competition for remaining resources. Being alone was getting to me that way. Floating around in my thoughts was also some notion that maybe the terrifying survivalist ninjas would take pity on me and adopt me as one of their own, teaching me to be silent, deadly, and cool. Possibly they could teach Vet not to be such a dumbass, as well.

All this was just more background noise to the surface thoughts, which concerned getting the goat into car without its legs going stiff and causing it to not fit through the door. I may not have made a single facial expression the entire time I was trying to accomplish this. Packing up the car was a mechanical process. If I started thinking about how ridiculous it was, I might start laughing and just never stop.

By the time it started to get dark, the car was packed. I had fed the dog out of a can and let the goat and chicken out to find their own dinner in the park. Keeping an eye on them while eating peanut butter straight out of the jar, I tried to feel like part of a long tradition of redheaded shepherd girls instead of a former New Yorker who wasn't entirely sure how a chicken worked. A long dress and a crook probably would have helped, but I didn't have one. I was still wearing my button-down shirt, dirty black cargo pants, and the white scarf that doubled as a dust mask. There is probably a rule somewhere that says shepherdesses don't wear pleather jackets. If not, there should be. It wasn't very picturesque, and besides that, anyone working in such a rural profession should be able to get ahold of a chunk of real cow skin.

In order to catch the chicken again, I ran after it until it cornered itself under a see-saw. It performed what I would soon learn was a totally normal hunkering pose and allowed me to pick it up. Chickens are weird. I thought about naming it, but I realized that sooner or later I may have to eat it and that just wouldn't be okay. Holding it at arm's length and referring to it as 'the chicken' made the situation at least a little more acceptable. I put the bird in the cage and the cage in the car. I was sad to leave my desk, but I figured if there was anyone else left in this stupid inexplicably-saved city, they might need it. It was time to go.

Driving is both easier and more fun when there's no one else on the road. This was very lucky, because I really had completely forgotten how to drive a car.

I alternated between hell-for-rubber speeding and doing the little old church lady creep, just because I had no sense of consistent gas pedal pressure. I felt off-center. Driving a moped, I was always supposed to be in the middle of the lane. This caused me to drive with my passenger side nudging the shoulder and freaked me right the hell out when I hit a rumble strip.

I was trying to head northeast, figuring that an attempt to get to Canada in a somewhat straight line would work out eventually. Navigating around the big crack in the city was like being a kid trying to solve the paper maze on a restaurant menu:

Straight, right, nope. Back up.

Straight, right, nope. Back into a telephone pole.

Straight, right . . .

Finally I found a street that had been affected only the tiniest bit. There was a gap about six inches wide running through my lane. Avoiding all speculation about geological instability, I bombed right over it and headed out of Portland.

After less than an hour of driving, I had to pull over because my knuckles had passed white and were turning blue. Vet was whining. I had forgotten how to blink like a normal person, and my contact lenses were turning into hard plastic bottle caps in my eyes. They were overnight lenses, but I was supposed to take them out once a week and let my eyes breathe. That hadn't exactly been happening. Even P.S., I'd been pretty slack about it. These contacts had probably been in my eyes since my last date with Fuckhead number . . . well, whatever number I had been up to.

I parked at a mall off the highway and leaned back in my seat. Facing facts wasn't any fun, but it had to be said that I'd never exactly had my shit together and been a responsible adult.

Vet tried to chew on the goat. It went rigid.

I swatted at him and wished he understood English.

The inside of the mall was really, really big. I'd never realized how big malls were before because they were always full of people. Looking down a quarter mile of sneakers and neon-colored kitchen appliances, I had two thoughts. The second one was *I do not want to be here.* Fortunately, it wasn't as fast as the first one: *I need better shoes.*

The mall was mostly intact, but a frozen yogurt shop had fallen into the outlet for my usual favorite shoe chain store, so I went towards the central shops and climbed over some fallen walkway into the largest department store. On the other side of the rubble, mannequins were lying everywhere, mostly dismembered. A plastic child's head with a sun hat on stared at me from behind a cash register. As soon as I shined the flashlight on it, I made a '*whaaahaaug*' noise that made the whole thing even eerier and then ran off into the store. I didn't stop until I hit the Juniors section. Even then, I hid inside a round clothes rack for a little while, trying to think of anything other than mannequins coming to life and screaming. My breathing slowly returned to normal. The mottled purple shirts surrounding me smelled like dye and detergent. I crawled out. When I turned the flashlight back on and played the white beam over the store, I saw that it wasn't such good shape as I had initially thought. Men's clothes had been obliterated. There was no way to get to the second floor. Not having my most coherent day ever, I believe what I said as I waved the flashlight around was, "Well. Hrmphh. Balls . . . Mm-Hm. Definitely balls." Even worse, it came out in my creaky, scratchy, vocal-chords-forgot-how-to-work voice. If I didn't get back on track, I was just going to stand right here in the skinny jeans and midriff hoodies until I went mad from the outside in.

I started tearing through clothes, looking for something practical.

Let me fucking tell you: There is no such thing as practical women's clothing in a department store. It's all a rainbow of polyester and gauze, jeans you can't circulate blood in and shirts that couldn't protect you from a light breeze. Don't even get me started on 'winter clothing.'

When is a jacket not a jacket? When it only comes down to your under-boob. When else is a jacket not a jacket? When it's see-through. Also, the seemingly immortal stereotype that women need a hundred pairs of shoes and will compulsively buy more . . . about that. I don't know how it started, but I know why it happens now: Most women's shoes can only be worn twenty or thirty times before they start to fall apart. Unless you want to run out of shoes every month or so, it's better to just keep a bazillion of them around so you have a back-up pair when you break a heel or your nice flats get wet and the whole piece of pleather covering your toe falls off.

All right, I guess I got myself started. But it needed to be said, damn it.

If there is a future where mankind reverts to cobblers and hand-making clothes from the ultimate scratch (which I think involves sheep, possibly plants), this is my edict handed down from history: Never make clothing this poorly again. Also, try not to group the hubs of civilization together on the very edges of tectonic plates. That was a bad idea.

Way in the back of women's shoes, past all the strappy useless stilettos and giant clunky wedges, I found a little shelf. There was a sign over it that said "For the working woman!" It was accompanied by a picture in which a brunette model, who looked incapable of lifting anything heavier than a Chihuahua, was wearing work boots and holding a decorative hammer. She looked very happy. Possibly because no one else in the history of the world has been paid what she was for standing around holding a hammer.

Under it, there were three types of boots. They were made of real leather. One of the display shoes, a steel-toed Doc Martin, was even in my size. Suddenly I was happy to be an average American shoe size. Otherwise, I would have had to find a back room and go digging, but as a size eight I just had to open the box under the display to get the other shoe. In my rush to put them on, I laced the non-display shoe all wrong, but it's not like anyone was going to care, so I just left if that way. I don't know how work boots are supposed to be laced. Possibly there are tools involved.

I thought about all the things I wanted to take out of

the mall, but picturing the size of the car put my material desire in check. Also, I thought the dog and the goat would probably kill each other if I left them for too long.

I took some boots.

On my way out, I took a big puffy jacket and kicked a mannequin in its creepy face.

I went to the movie theater.

Looking at posters for movies I would never see made me sad.

I found a trash bag full of stale popcorn, well-preserved in the plastic.

I took it with me, thinking the chicken might eat it.

Now I have to talk about the geese.

On my way out of the mall, I was walking through a section under the skylights when I heard a noise. I didn't really have time to get a good panic attack going before I realized it was birds in the rafters. Jays and starlings are not very threatening. The deer that I encountered on my way out the door was a good deal more startling, but it ran. Wildlife was taking over where the humans had left off. Such convenient shelters we'd built! And, at least for a while, such good unattended food sources.

There was a goose in the parking lot. Just one. It wasn't so very out of place, really, since the mall was right near a small lake. I broke open the huge plastic bag and threw it some popcorn. The goose ate it and honked. I threw some more. It was almost fun.

Then more geese waddled up over the edge of the parking lot. One tentative honk became an onslaught of war-cries, with more muppety-looking birds swinging their tail feathers on the parking lot every second. Soon there were thirty of them. The lead goose flapped its giant wings at me and charged.

Hwoooonk!

In hindsight, I could probably have taken those geese with my bare hands. They bite and they smack you with their wings but they've got long, vulnerable necks and little tiny brains. If I'd let Vet out of the car, he probably would have killed all of them.

Or he would have gotten his ass kicked, maybe lost an eye.

At any rate, I now understand that I was not in mortal danger from a flock of ten pound birds. I have to say that I knew that before I explain what I actually did:

EEEEIIIIIIIIIIIIIIIAAAAAAAAAAAH!

I can't perfectly transcribe the noise I made as I launched the hefty bag of popcorn into the air and ran for the car, but I think that gives the right general impression. Eeeeiiiiiiiiiiiiiiiaaaaaaaaah.

Unfortunately, some of the geese were not the least bit distracted by the flying popcorn and pursued me all the way to the Subaru. Doubly unfortunate was the fact that I had locked the door.

I circled the car at a dead run three times before the geese stopped chasing me and just stood around flapping their wings, creepy little tongues hanging out, making occasional hissing sounds. I flattened myself against the door and tried to unlock the car. When I finally managed to open the door, Vet stuck his head out and promptly got his nose bitten by a goose, which scared both of them back a few feet and allowed me to dive into the great hulking fort of the Subaru. One of the geese started to wade forward and I kicked it in the chest so I could slam the door without scooping it into the car with us.

The geese ate their popcorn. I decided that, when the packaged, processed food ran out, I was going to get some kind of range weapon and learn to hunt geese. Fuck geese. I was going to become a Great Goose Hunter.

I looked apologetically at the chicken and fed it some of the parrot food from the pet store, then poured out enough bottled water for my whole weird road-trip crew. The goat seemed to be all about the parrot food, so I gave him some, too. I ate some more peanut butter. All of this was done in autopilot adrenaline mode. As soon as I ran out of useful things to do, I sighed and thumped my head on the steering wheel, honking the horn with my eyebrow.

The geese did not fly away. They replied to the car.

Honk.

I put some antibiotic cream on Vet's nose, which he immediately licked off again with his pink slobbery dog tongue. We repeated this process several times. Eventually, I realized that no effort of mine was going to keep him from licking his own nose and that really, all I was doing was feeding him antibiotic cream. I fed him some jerky instead. We all settled down to sleep in the car. I kind of needed to pee, but I wasn't facing the geese again and I just couldn't add to the horrible smells already building up inside the Subaru.

Sooner or later, this dog and I were going to need a lot more meat. I didn't know how to get any. I knew that the deer, the geese, the chicken, and probably even the goat were technically animals that got eaten by humans, but I couldn't begin to fathom the process by which a live animal eying me balefully became a lump of edible stuff you could put on top of rice and smother in barbecue sauce. *But damn, if any animal ever deserved it*, I thought, *it's those fucking evil geese.* I resolved to try to kill one in the morning. Then I scrunched up in the driver's seat and went to sleep.

Of course, when the sun came up, the geese were gone. After a good morning pee and breakfast all around, with some decorative mall garden grazing for the goat, I was out of little missions. As far as I was concerned, it was next stop, Canada.

It could never have been quite that simple. But at the time, the sun was rising, I was fed, the dog was happy, I had some semblance of a roof over my head, and everything seemed easy and good. So, that's how it was, to me. Next stop, Canada.

CHAPTER FIVE
POST-APOCALYPSE TRANSPORTATION, PART A

Cars are amazing. I don't know if mankind will still have them in the future, the poor post-apocalyptic bastards, but cars are just amazing. They have wheels and a roof and you can fit a dog and a goat and a chicken and a human in them and still have room for a good forty pounds of food. I love cars. On the second day of the road trip, I came to love cars for a whole new reason. They play music.

After wobbling along an entire mile or so of road where the pavement was cracked and broken, and most of the buildings on either side had fallen down, I started looking frantically for more houses. A gas station appeared to have exploded and was still smoking in a thick, greasy plume. For a few miles, I was afraid that I had run out of things to plunder. As soon as there were standing buildings again, I stopped anywhere that looked promising. I broke into a peach-colored house with smooth plaster columns on the front porch, looking for additional food and water because we were running low. In this particular house, I found a bunch of canned soup and some mix tapes. They were labeled things like "Work-Out Mix," "From CD for

Car," and "Jazz Babes." They looked new. I didn't even know you could still buy audio cassettes, but suddenly it made sense to me that the mix tape was not dead because, for years, cars had been made with tape players, and lots of people were still driving those cars. Since I was currently one of them, maybe even the only one remaining, I took the tapes.

Back in the car, I popped in "Jazz Babes." The tape player clicked and ground for a minute, and then started playing music. Music!

"Mayhem, do-di-do, Oh-woh-oh, yeah!"

I didn't know the song, but halfway through I started singing along anyway. Mayhem. Oh, yeah.

Vet took to howling along with the tape as we bombed down the Eighty-Four. The goat was not happy about this. My driving skills, such as they had ever been, were really coming back to me by the time we came shooting out the other side of The Dalles and the Columbia River Highway abruptly became more river than highway. I have never stomped so hard, or done *anything* so hard, as I did that day trying to brake before the road ended in a twist of rebar and rock. I very nearly broke my own leg.

The roads were a mess down by the river, but that may actually have saved me. Every time the car hit a branch or skewed on the gravel, it was one more thing between me and plummeting into the river. It didn't seem that way to me, of course. I was bumping and rocketing towards a very severe end of the road, and even starting at thirty miles an hour and being slowed down by debris, the only thing I could think at that time was *OH MY GOD WHY WON'T THIS CAR STOP?* I screamed it out loud.

The seat belt clamped down. Dash lights blurred in

front of me, jittering and weaving. I strained my legs and neck trying not to get thrown around in the car. The Subaru's fat ass swung around either side of the lane. For brief seconds, I had a giant dog in my lap, because there are some situations where having four legs but no opposable thumbs just isn't the ideal configuration. For some delusional half-second, I felt like even the car itself was panicking, trying to flail, and was probably going to choke on the mix tape.

If I had been going faster, I would have gone over the edge. Instead, most of the terrifying aspects of the experience originated from the fact that I had freaked out, trying to swerve away and slamming on the brakes at the same time.

When something very, very bad is happening, time does not really slow down, but sometimes there just a second or two for really clear thought.

The highway here was a narrow strip with the blue-gray river on one side and a wall of tan rock on the other. I knew I was panicking on the outside, but the end result was that I slowed the car down and then rather gently plowed it into the rock wall head-on, which, under the circumstances, was the smartest thing I could possibly have done. This considered, my last thought before I hit the cliff face was *Ha! I'm bloody brilliant*!

Then I bounced my head off of the steering wheel and the driver's side window, consecutively. Vet ended up in a pile in the passenger side foot well. When I shook my head and looked back to check on the rest of the gang, the chicken was hunkered down in its wire cage and looking at me with accusation in its beady black eyes. The goat did not seem to have noticed that anything had happened. It was chewing on a seat belt. Two of its legs had gone rigid, but that was nothing out of the ordinary.

I hesitated before turning off the car. If it didn't start again, we were all in big trouble. On the other hand, if the car exploded, we were in even bigger trouble. I turned the key and took it out of the ignition, holding it out in front of me like something precious but dangerous. A poisoned Faberge egg, maybe, or a rock star boyfriend. Never has a car key been the subject of such delicate consideration.

Vet rolled over in the foot well and made a sighing sound. When I got out of the car, he jumped out after me and I checked him over for injury. His nose was still bloody and scratched up from the goose bite, and there was a hardening lump between his ears like he'd head-butted the glove box on his way to the floor. He let me touch the tender spot but he clearly wasn't happy about it. I relented. I wasn't sure I had the common sense to gauge whether or not I'd broken my dog, but I didn't know what I'd do about it even if I had. Vet started to chew on my pant leg. He was probably okay.

The car looked substantially worse off than the dog. Both headlights were now obliterated. The hood had one great kink in it, all the way across, so that it was now more of an engine tent. The passenger side mirror, scraped off when I sideswiped the rock wall, glittered in pieces fifty yards back up the road. Both sides of the car's body were crinkled from nose to doors, and the passenger door made a sad creaking noise when I opened it and then refused to close again. I was lucky the car had four of the damn things.

I almost stuck my hand under the fold in the hood to touch the engine, but stopped when my fingertips told me the air around it was scalding. I wasn't exactly sure what I was trying to do. Maybe I wanted to touch the engine to reassure myself that it was still there, or perhaps I thought patting the spark plugs reassuringly was going to comfort the car. Both of these were pretty stupid, but what can I say? Sometimes we drink out of the paint glass. Sometimes we come inches from reaching into the running garbage disposal. People get sidetracked.

The back hatch of the car still worked. I opened it to get a can of soup and found the goat with its head stuck over the seat, having nudged aside the plywood and eaten through the plastic bags to get to more parrot food. I was starting to reconsider the goat. Maybe you could milk one, and probably you could eat one, but I was personally too uninformed and ill-equipped to do either of these things except under the most dire circumstances, and there was still enough beef-and-potato soup left to last me for weeks.

While I ate my soup, I meandered over the edge of the broken road, trying to be casual but feeling like I might at any moment start yelling and kicking things into the river. Damn the Interstate! Damn it for not being there when I needed it, and for scaring me! Damn it for trying to kill me! Especially that last one, I think. That was definitely the last straw. This highway and I needed to have a talk. We were breaking up. I was going to go find myself a nice side road, one that would be reliable and kind to me.

Below me, the river was not only full of tumbling debris and ash, but was also steaming. An eddy had formed in the hole where the highway used to be. Water was churning around the hunks of concrete, and I didn't register the steam at first because it was easily confused for the normal mist of water trying to run and tripping instead. After a minute of leaning over it, I noticed that I was warm. There was no cold refreshing spray of ashy river water. There was actual condensation on my forehead, in my hair, collecting in my ears. I went to the north side of the road and looked downriver.

The whole thing was steaming, just a little bit.

Suddenly it seemed uncomfortably warm standing there on the road. My imagination ran away with possibilities of how such a large volume of water was heated enough to vaporize. Finally my brain arrived at an image of my teakettle on the stove. I wasn't sure that the heat source was nearby, but I did not want to be within a hundred miles when the earth started to whistle. There was an abnormal smell in the air, and it might have been from the car, but at that moment I swore it was sulfur or some other underground hell-smell that was never supposed to be detectable from I-84.

The sky was getting dark again, but the sun was still a diffuse glow directly centered in the sky. This patch of the Northwest was being cheated out of some prime daylight hours by a massive cloud bank. I swiveled my head around, taking in everything around me, and realized that I didn't need any special training to read the natural signs of Something Really Bad Coming.

The colors of the world were shifting. I could feel the sky on my skin. Cloud banks were marching like ashen armies. Every tiny peach-fuzz follicle on my whole body woke up at the same time. On top of all of those warning signs, my faithful canine companion finally proved his worth by howling his bleeding idiot head off, trying to let me know that I, the human, needed to do something *right now.*

Somewhere way back in this, I mentioned how 'instantaneous' in geological time can mean 'over the course of a couple weeks.' Vet and I knew something was going wrong, but it was happening a hell of a lot slower than our brains are really set up to handle. When it comes to animals (humans included), something bad is either about to happen to us or it isn't. We were right in that something bad was about to happen to us, but it was happening in more of a geological than an animal kind of time frame. Something horrible was starting to happen right now. In this case, 'right now' didn't arrive for a few hours, by which time I had successfully restarted the car and was thirty miles down Route 197.

This would have been extremely lucky, if the geological notion of 'right here' was more precise than its definition of 'right now.' It wasn't. As far as Mount Hood was concerned, I might as well not have moved. To a mountain, 'right here' is defined by what you can see from the top.

As far as I was concerned, I had put myself in exactly the worse possible place to be when Mount Hood started erupting: Due east and downhill, right in its path.

The first signs went completely unnoticed. Vet and I were howling along to the mix tape, doing a respectable fifteen miles an hour down the highway. I was preoccupied. I was swerving around bits of nature and sometimes bits of furniture which I assumed had fallen off of people's cars when they tried to evacuate. Paint cans had splattered on the highway. My window was rolled down so I could listen to the engine. I also kept an eye on the engine temperature gauge, because I knew you were supposed to, though the rest of my knowledge on the subject was that the needle should probably stay away from the red part. Looking back on it, I guess I knew what I needed to know. The goat was alternately head-butting the back of my seat and making loud goat noises. Vet was losing patience and started snapping at it. The hair on his back was all puffed up and had been that way since I-84.

The engine temperature started going up, so I pulled off the highway and ended up in the parking lot of the

Tygh Valley General Store. It seemed like a nice, safe, out of the way place to think about engine temperatures. I knew that 'coolant' was a thing, and that it went . . . somewhere, and that it was probably leaking like a bastard from my run-in with the rock wall.

I raided the general store with the ease and joy of a new habit. There was still beef jerky galore, for which both the dog and I would be very grateful later, but the sight and overwhelming smell of corn dogs left out to rot put me off the idea of eating for the time being. I let the animals out of the car and put in the new supplies. When I freed the chicken, I noticed that there were actually three eggs in the bottom of the cage (two whole and one broken) and I got all excited. Chickens lay eggs! I had done something smart after all. The store had some hunting supplies, which included fire starters, so I made a little cooking fire and scrambled myself some eggs in the bottom of my pot. It felt a little weird doing this in front of the chicken, but the bird didn't seem to mind and was otherwise occupied trying to scratch bugs out of the driveway. I fed it some corn. Vet was still upset and puffed up, but he was happy to share some of the scrambled eggs anyway. The goat started to wander off, but I figured I could catch it later. Catching a fainting goat is not hard. After getting the car book out, I went back to my lunch.

I jumped up on the roof of the Subaru, wedged myself in next to the moped, and settled down to read. The pot of scrambled eggs balanced nicely on my lap. There were still clouds, but it wasn't raining. Things could be worse.

By the time I was pouring water into my car as stopgap coolant, things got worse.

Most of Mount Hood was visible from my car. Just for reference, Mount Hood is visible from most of the state of Oregon. It was one of the highest points in the continental United States, back when there was such a thing. Mount Hood was a National Forest all by itself. More than a hundred people had died climbing it. There was snow on it year round. At least, there had been snow, up until now.

While I had my head stuck under the broken car hood, which I had to wrench up and then hold by hand, I was focused on looking for a coolant leak. When you don't know anything about cars, but you open one up and get in there anyway, it's like sticking your head in the lion's mouth. I was intent on not screwing it up. I didn't see a leak, and there was nothing on the ground, so I topped it off with water and screwed the cap back on as hard as I could. Maybe the engine was just running hot because it was so warm outside. I didn't notice Mount Hood until I'd wedged the hood of the car back into place and smacked the dent with a crowbar for good measure. Then I looked up.

The mountain was gently smoking. When anything eleven thousand feet tall smokes, no matter how gently, a person eventually takes notice.

I wondered how many small earthquakes I hadn't noticed because I was driving.

"Vet. Vet, get in the car. Get in the car. *Vet-get-in-the-car-right-now!*"

The dog was so low on his belly he might as well have burrowed into the ground. The chicken had flown into the car at the first sign of me freaking out, figuring its cage was a place of food, water, and safety, but Vet did not want to move. He wasn't even blinking, just growling continuously. An earthquake started. It was bigger than the ones I'd felt before.

I felt like all my internal organs were vibrating independently of each other. That wasn't the weirdest of the sensations, but it's the only one I can describe properly. The rest of the experience was all about hearing a sound through your feet and gravity getting drunk, which doesn't make any god damn sense at all.

I couldn't think of anything smart to do, so I laid down next to the dog and watched the mountain, trying to figure how much of what I was seeing was Mount Hood shaking and how much of it was my eyeballs vibrating in my head.

At first, it looked like someone was drawing a line down the mountain with a pencil. Echoing across Oregon was a sound like miles of cracking whips. Then another line appeared, and the entire area between them was sliding down towards me. Ash and mud were venting out of the sides, and an opaque plume was now shooting straight up into the air over the mountain. The clouds were parting overhead, rushing away in a perfect ring to make room for hot air and volcanic pyrocumulus.

The mudslide was getting closer, and now I could even hear it rushing down the mountain. Earthquake or no earthquake, the time to go was at least sixty seconds ago. Somehow, I managed to pick up the big panic-stricken dog, throw him into the car, get the key in the ignition, and drive, tearing away on the Sherars Bridge Highway through the middle of nowhere. The general store had fallen down as soon as I'd pulled out of the parking lot, taking the fetid corndogs with it, and I was racing the intensified shaking of the road, just barely pulling ahead of the land wave. I refused to look in the rear view mirror, but I could still see it out of the corner of my eye. A fifth of Mount Hood was chasing me down the highway. I had a head start, but it was a hell of a lot faster.

There was a small bridge ahead, bucking and twisting in ways that a road just shouldn't do, but I knew it was less risky than staying to get buried by a mountain so I roared across it. I made it thirty miles in twenty-five minutes. I would have made it faster, but there were periods of time where the tires bounced right off the shaking ground. The car started to smoke. The initial earthquake seemed to be over, but the moving mountain was still sending vibrations far and wide. The engine temperature starting shooting up again and instead of stopping, I tried to hit the gas even harder because I might as well use the car to get as far away from the volcano as I could while it was still functioning. If I blew us up, I blew us up. The landslide was falling behind.

When the highway suddenly went from long straight stretches to the abrupt corners of civilization, I was not expecting it. I tried to brake but the car spun, throwing Vet into the back, and we plowed into a house. The windshield shattered into my lap, the high crunch of glass cracking in contrast to the low crunches of the earth moving. My seat belt became a blunt instrument. The roof of the house fell on the car. Light brown shingles covered the passenger seat.

To this day, I'm not entirely sure if I passed out or if I just gave up on the whole day and fell asleep. It seems possible. Me, strapped in to a suicidal Subaru in some stranger's living room, with a lap full of windshield . . . Bed time for Queen Mab of the Broken Glass.

I do not know how I managed to do all of that. I still swear that I could not possibly have lifted that damn dog, or driven that fast, or crashed that badly without dying. I just know that I did, and that I ask the universe every day to never, ever make me do it again.

Mount Hood tried to kill me, and I survived, but I also lost the goat. I like to think that the poor goat is okay out there somewhere, that it ran away from the volcano and spent its days wild and free, eating from the long-gone suburbanite's gardens that now overgrew their decorative bounds and went to seed whenever they felt like it. I hope that's what really happened to the goat. I never saw it again.

I still do not know how to milk a goat.

But I am much better at driving a car.

CHAPTER SIX
FIRST AID: YOU NEVER KNOW UNTIL YOU (ALMOST) DIE

I remember waiting to open my eyes.

There was a little light coming through my eyelids, and I knew that if I looked I was going to be able to see whatever was in front of me, and that what was in front of me might be my own mangled body, or a dead dog, or possibly a chicken impaled on a piece of windshield. It even occurred to me that maybe someone had been in this living room when I got here. Wow . . . 'got here' makes it sound like I sauntered in to the house in a totally normal way, rather than ramming the living room with a ton and a half of exploding car. At any rate.

My method of 'getting here' left the possibility of a homeowner's corpse on my hugely fucked-up hood, and that just added to the list of things I did not want to see right now. I sat there with my eyes closed for a long time, assessing my pains and trying to go back to sleep.

Eventually, the chicken said "Bwa*ruk*," and I knew I would have to get up . . . for the sake of the chicken, if nothing else. You can't just leave chickens in the back of

Subarus to die. If I did that, I would never be able to look at myself again. I wasn't sure that I even wanted to look at myself now, but that was beside the point. The chicken might have a concussion or something, though it was probably very hard to tell with chickens.

I opened my eyes.

Sometimes, people get into very minor car accidents and end up snapping their necks, or slicing open their jugular on the only broken window in the whole car. This was not one of those times.

This was the other kind, where the accident looks like everyone should have been killed, but instead everyone is standing around next to the waiting but unneeded emergency vehicles, starring wide-eyed at their car and saying, "What just happened? Why am I not dead?" This was the kind that gets reported in the papers with the words, "All passengers miraculously survived." There were no newspapers left, but I kind of wish there had been, because I thought being miraculously unharmed was a pretty decent thing to get locally famous for. I would, however, have to ask them to let me clean up before they took my picture. I was not looking my best.

'Miraculously survived' is not the same as 'totally fine.' It mostly means 'should have been dead.'

There was a large spidered plate of crushed safety glass in my lap. Shards from the edges were all over, inside the folds and weaves of my clothes. I wanted to shake my hair out, but considering what my hair contained, shaking it all over myself and the car wouldn't have been the smart course of action. All of my body parts moved, but they all hurt. My right foot seemed to be calling for my attention louder than anything else. When I tried to focus on it, I realized two things: I may have broken my foot, and I had definitely lost a contact lens.

When Vet heard me shuffling around in my seat, he climbed into the front with me and started nosing my face to see if I was okay. He stepped on my lap. I screamed a little and tried to push him into the back again, before he could start trying to help by chewing on my messed-up toes.

I couldn't see out of one eye. Breathing was a challenge it had never been before. My foot was suffering. I had to get to Canada, and I wasn't sure how to get out of the car. Still, true adaptation to the new world had begun. I didn't even wish for anyone to rescue me. There were no more phones, no more ambulances, no more good friends who would save my ass when I did stupid things. All those P.S. conveniences seemed more like wishes I'd once had than things that had been a reality only a month or two ago, so I started trying to figure it out on my own, and tried the door handle.

Car doors do not open when you crush them. They also don't open when there are hundreds of pounds of house in the way.

We were lucky, though, because the ass end of the Subaru was still sticking out of the living room, mooning the world. I was able to open the back hatch. The dog barreled out on his own, then turned circles in the yard and immediately lay down again. Rather than try to stand and lift things, I just started shoving my gear out of the car from the inside, sitting with my foot propped up on the dash and shoveling food out the back with my frame pack. It was an awkward job. A can of sausages hit Vet between the ears and, after his initial shock, he started chewing on it. Packages broke open on the ground. The chicken huddled away from me in its cage, probably wondering if I was going to launch its poor battered bird body out of the car as well.

I would have to take the chicken out a little more gently. First, I had to get myself out, which was not going to be fun. My arms were failing and my foot was presenting a serious problem. My head rolled around on a neck that felt like a coffee straw. I needed to rest. Thinking back to times in my life when I'd actually done physical labor instead of blogging and studying all day, I grabbed a random food item from the bottom of the car and ate it, knowing that when I woke up I would need the energy. The car smoked and steamed, darkening the view of the front living room. I watched it go black. Then I fell asleep for another three hours with a mouth full of granola bar.

By the time I woke up, the dog had jumped back into the car and laid his head on my lap, and the last bit of granola bar had turned to glue in my mouth. I drank some water and got to work.

I should have thought about the order in which I did things. If I had, I would have done them differently, but there was still a lot of P.S. stupidity left in me, so I spent half an hour wincing, unpacking, and trying to haul my moped off the car and out of the debris before it finally occurred to me to do something about my foot. By the time I realized I had some body tending to do, my foot was so swollen that I couldn't get my bootlaces loose to do anything about it. I sat down in the very back of the cleared-out Subaru with my survival and first aid books. Time to get some reading done.

Ash was falling from the sky again. I looked at Vet. Against my better judgment, I spent the better part of an hour trying to get him to understand that he should drag a tarp over the food and the moped. He encouraged my efforts by showing his best signs of intelligence, such as spanking the ground with his paws, tilting his head in a listening attitude, and whining pathetically. When I thought he understood, I pointed to the tarp and said, "Go get it!"

Vet, doing his doggie best to make me happy, leaped onto the tarp. He got a face full of ash when it puffed out and nearly suffocated himself, sneezed so vigorously I was afraid he was actually having a seizure, and then attacked the tarp with the conviction and skill of a great warrior seeking vengeance. More ash puffed up, and Vet repeated this process several times before shredding the tarp to bits and then running back to me, wagging his tail, to share with me his victory. I wanted to cry, but if I did he would lick my face. I dragged myself out of the car and hopped around on one foot, putting the remaining pieces of tarp over my things as best I could. When the largest bit covering the moped started to blow away, Vet caught it and ripped it into even smaller pieces. I started to wonder if life would have been better if I'd saved the goat and left the dog behind, instead.

Until Vet started whining. Then my heart was suddenly breaking for that damn dog. He rolled over beside the car wreckage, his fur turning grey with ash, sneezing and whimpering. There was blood on his nose. I panicked and hauled him into the car with me. If I describe the look he gave me once he was in there beside me, I'm going to cry, so I refuse . . . but anyone who's ever met a dog knows the look just fine. It says, "I want to die, and you can make it all better, but it's okay if you don't; I'll totally understand if you're busy or something." It also says that the damn dog loves you, and is still going to love you if you leave him in a ditch somewhere.

Dogs. Oh my god, dogs. Right?

I rinsed his nose with a little water and a tee shirt from the book store. Once I cleared off the ash, I could see that both the scratch from the goose and the inside of his nose were bleeding. Without taking the time to consult any more of the first aid book, I hobbled into action.

Inside my backpack was the bag of goodies from the department store pharmacy. Between that and my purse, I had some useful stuff. More antibiotic cream for the top of Vet's nose seemed like a priority. I put some on, then grabbed his tongue every time he tried to lick it. It was a funny process, but it made me tear up. My dog. I had broken my dog.

Once we were done playing the tongue-grabbing game, I rinsed his face off a little more and shined my flashlight in his nose. Still bleeding. I wasn't sure what to do about that so I tried to hold the rag shirt on it. Vet sneezed again. He started panting and drooling. He looked like he was about to fall asleep, but couldn't get comfortable. I started bawling for real then, because Vet was mine, and dogs die, and I couldn't think of a single thing to do.

Animals are much better at healing themselves without medical care than humans are. Vet had inhaled a lot of ash and given himself a nosebleed, and probably had a good headache, but he was going to be fine. I spent the whole night tending to him in back of the Subaru while sticking my foot in the air, propped up over the seat, trying to get the swelling to go down. Eventually we both fell asleep. In the morning, Vet had some blood crusted on his face but he was smiling at me and making mad dashes between my lap and the food pile, a dog clearly in good order and wanting sausages. I dragged myself around, feeding and watering the dog, the chicken, and myself, and then woke up enough to deal with the current problem. The dog was fine. I was not. I had to get to Canada, but I was in the middle of nowhere with no car, a big pile of gear, one contact lens, and a broken foot.

I wish I had something witty to say about it, but I don't.

The first aid book said that I should cut off my boot. The thought of sawing through my precious leather foot-armor made me balk. It's not like I had another pair handy. I resolved to keep my boot on and think of it like a bandage, but once I had been on my feet for five minutes I had to stop. The boot had to come off, and I had to find out what I had done to myself. I just couldn't do it. I couldn't give up my boots. Even if I could, I was probably going to stab myself in the foot trying to cut through them. I lay on the ground with my foot up on the car. It was over. I was just going to die here. While I was laying around waiting to die, I had an epiphany and decided I might live instead.

I cut the bootlaces. I took the boot off. I thought, *Fucking DUH.*

Chasing Vet away from my foot was a challenge. When a dog sees an injury, his strongest and most immediate desire in the world is to lick it, because that will make it better. In the evolutionary sense, it seems to have worked for them, but I wasn't willing to gamble on the method's efficacy on humans. Also, having him plow his head into my broken foot trying to lick it would hurt like hell. After three or four attempts, he laid down and harrumphed.

I tried to peel off my sock, but ended up having to make a score mark in the ankle and tear it instead. I used only my fingertips. The sock, not in great condition even before it had been soaked in blood, had become a semi-solid mass of cotton and various body bits. Suddenly I desperately did not want to see what was under it. It was going to be bad. Probably also sticky.

I poured a little water from the nearest bottle over my toes. It should have been cold, or at least unpleasantly wet and squishy, but for a minute I didn't feel anything and that worried me a great deal. Then it worked its way through the sock and the blood. It stung. I started whining. The dog started whining. The process was far from fun, but the sock was loosening up. Using just the very tips of my fingernails, I peeled it off. When I looked at my foot, I passed through feelings of heat, dizziness, and nausea before just passing out entirely.

I had to deal with it, obviously. When I came to, I drank a little water and tried to think of it as someone else's foot. That didn't help, so I tried to think of it as a really realistic horror movie prop, which was what it resembled most closely.

The thing that was hardest to look at and the thing that was most wrong were two different deals. My second and third toes had been smashed into the steel toe of my boot so hard that they had squished like the world's most disgusting bath beads. They hurt, but in the grand scheme of my currently totally fucked up life, they weren't so big a deal. They were just toes. Doctors don't even put casts on them if you break them.

But there, a little farther up, was a tremendously painful dent. It was centered on my foot and bruising and swelling already radiated from it, down to the toes and halfway up my ankle. It looked like a bee had somehow stung me from the inside, and I was having the weirdest and worst allergic reaction ever. I had fractured a bone. And then I had ignored it and walked around on it all morning.

Before doing anything sensible, I went through every reaction known to twenty-something womankind. I cursed, cursed louder, rolled my eyes, waved my hands around, wished for an alcoholic drink, dug the cigarettes out of my bag and smoked three, gagged a little, cried a lot, and screamed in frustration. I was almost glad that the rest of humankind was gone, because if someone had come along and found me like this it probably would have been the most mortifying event of my life. I may or may not have punched the car.

Then I consulted my first aid book, wrapped my foot tightly in clean, improvised shirt-bandages, and got on with my life. Slowly.

My foot wasn't the only damage, but I was having trouble getting a real inventory on how the rest of me was doing. It seemed like the best thing to do would be to just lay down and die. Of course, instinct denies us that course of action. Even when giving up really would be the most sensible plan, the most basic of the evolved brain systems comes to haunt us: Eat, sleep, move, fight, live. Damn it. At least I managed to get some higher brain functions into the mix and find the best ways to get it done.

Using a debarked tree branch for an awkward crutch, I started hobbling around the little town I'd crashed into. The houses were all painted in the inoffensive spectrum of temperate climate camouflage. The most vibrant color among them was a sickly yellow. Most were surrounded by rusting cars and scrap metal. In one back yard, I found a kiddie pool, sheltered from the ashfall by a free-standing corrugated tin roof that also protected a tractor and a child's bicycle. The four-by-fours holding it up looked stable enough. It wasn't a spa, but I was happy to find it.

I stripped down, a process that went smoothly above

the waist but was complicated by my mangled foot when it came to pants. I fumbled and winced. I laid down on the ground and went through a very slow wiggling process to get my pants off without injuring myself further, which worked. When I had managed to shed everything, I started to ease myself into the little plastic pool. This is exactly the sort of thing where overestimating one's own strength becomes a problem.

I started out by lowering myself gently, slippery hands shaking on the edges of the pool, and ended up giving out at the elbows and crashing, my ass falling hard on the faces of the smiling cartoon penguins that covered the bottom. The plastic creaked. I sighed, and started washing myself off.

Quite a bit of the horror show that was my body turned out to just be special effects. There was a lot of blood where there weren't actually wounds. What might have been bruises proved to be ash smudges. I used my hands to scrub my right leg, sticking out of the pool, and stopped where the swelling started. A wet bandage would only add to my problems. The water was warm enough to enjoy.

Rinsing off my face was tricky. I had to close my eyes for a long time to keep from filling them with ash, dirt, and blood. I gently poked and prodded, discovering some cuts on my head, painful only when touched. When I felt something small and alien in my eyebrow, my fingertips explored it for a second before I realized it was a piece of glass embedded in my face. It was slippery but I used my nails and managed to pull it out, frowning. I couldn't open my eyes, but for some reason I really wanted to see the thing that had just come out of my head. I reached out and blindly set it beside the kiddie pool for later examination.

Most of me, once clean, felt reasonably intact. The

water smelled like iron and soot, but I no longer wanted to just lay down and die. At least, not until I tried to wash my hair.

My hair is red, curly, long, and it hates me. It hated me even when I gave it top-shelf organic shampoo and conditioner every day, and would demonstrate its eternal anger by manifesting knots, poofs, and dreadlocks. Individual hairs would leap off my head at the first opportunity, leaving me with a ginger pillow and a shower drain that appeared to be on fire. It ate combs. Brushes bounced. The depictions of my hair type in beauty magazines would sometimes make me laugh until I bordered on hysterics. Some people think that having this classic Irish Girl hair is desirable, adding an air of unique mystery and class to any head. Well, it's time for another edition of "Let Me Fucking Tell You," because let me fucking tell you, nobody wants this hair. Having long curly red hair is mostly about fighting with it every day while suffering jokes about gingers having no soul and inappropriate comments about whether the carpet matches the drapes. This is not a desirable thing.

And it is *most definitely* not a thing that I wanted to be trying to wash apocalyptic debris out of in a kiddie pool, without shampoo, while trying to support the weight of my own mangled body.

When the dog came into the yard, he sniffed me and sneezed all over my head. This did not assist me in any way.

Once upon a time, my hair and I had a stable but lopsided relationship. I loved it, and it hated me, but as long as I was properly subservient we managed to get along. Now, my hair and I had officially crossed over into domestic abuse on both sides. It was time to end this disaster. I was going to solve my hair problems by cutting it off.

Clearly my brain was turning to mud.

I spent a few extra minutes soaking in my penguin-decorated tub before I could be bothered to get up, but finally I flailed my way out of the pool. There was another reference book I had failed to heed, one I read in high school. It was *Hitchhiker's Guide to the Galaxy.* The one rule from *Hitchhiker's Guide* was to always have a towel. I failed in this, and now I had to find something to wipe my face on so that I could open my damn eyes.

The dog ran up and knocked me over, right onto my foot. I howled. He howled. I laughed and I cried, and I could hear him doing a rolling-in-the-dirt dance, making happy harrumphing noises. There was a splash as he jumped in and out of the pool. I got up and staggered around, blind, injured, naked, hands out, trying to find the house that was right in front of me, dripping bloody, ashy water. I was the Creature from the Penguin Lagoon.

Finally, I touched the house. The plastic siding was gritty with road dirt. I groped around for a window and found one that was, in a rare case of my extreme good fortune, already open. I called out, but no one answered, so I tipped myself over the windowsill and landed on the floor in a shower of old paint chips. Vet jumped in and landed on me, then walked off. His nails clicked on the floor.

I bumped against a couch and grabbed a pillow to wipe my eyes. Nylon tassels tickled my neck.

The ability to see improved my life considerably. Finding a bathroom by feel wouldn't have been easy. Squinting and dripping my way around the house, I opened doors until I found one.

The people who lived here had clearly evacuated, but a few useful items were left behind and I employed them.

They included a ratty towel advertising beer, a guest toothbrush in a drawer, and a stash of the kind of cheap hair combs that photography companies give out on school picture day. Feeling much cleaner and more optimistic, I tried running one of these through my hair. It was a mistake. The comb was promptly eaten by my tortured and vengeful ginger mane.

I hobbled to the kitchen and found some scissors in a drawer.

Then I removed most of my hair, taking it from the 1960's to the 1920's in just three or four dozen easy steps. The collection of apocalyptic debris fell to the floor around me in a ring of fire. I was, in some small and stupid way, free.

An hour later, Vet and I were back at the demolished car. I had given my clothes a good dunking in the pool and wrung them out, then put them back on hoping to dry them out with my body heat. The scarf hung around my shoulders and stuck to my jacket, making an occasional sucking sound on the pleather. Vet licked my pant leg. His tongue was ashy. When I tried to shoo him away, he gave me a giant dog grin and started licking my hand instead. I surrendered to this secondary bath.

When I added the bonus supplies scored from the house with the pool, my pile of stuff was pretty intimidating. It was way more than I could carry, and even if I found another car, I didn't think I would be able to drive very well with my left foot. Bicycles were even further out of the question. My moped survived the wreckage, but again, it wouldn't carry everything.

There were a lot of junk cars around. I limped up and down the street, eyeballing the yards full of rusting bodies and empty wheel wells. There was one car in a driveway that looked like it might have been someone's actual usable vehicle, so I broke in and found the keys, but when I tried to start it absolutely nothing happened. I opened the hood. There was no engine. *Well*, I thought, *that explains why they didn't take it with them.* I did the broken-foot hokey-pokey hobble back to my moped.

There is a question, sometimes used to profile people's personalities, about a house on fire. *If your house were burning down, what would you take out first?* Many people would say pets, or books. Increasingly, they would say computers, which is completely understandable because in the last of the P.S. years the home computer had become a repository of all things: It was work, play, mail, movie collection, photo album, and music library. Given a chance, I probably would have taken mine from my house, just in case there was ever electricity again. To think that the music of Amanda Palmer, or the movie *Cabaret* might be gone forever . . . I just couldn't stand it.

The question facing me now was a little different.

The whole world is on fire. What do I take with me?

Whatever I could fit on a moped.

I could probably take a lot of my medical supplies, but not everything, so I had to use what I could right then. I sat down with my reference books and my pharmacy bag to learn about saving my own life.

Almost half of the prescription drugs I had taken from the department store pharmacy turned out to be antibiotics. I considered this very lucky. The end of the world had come close enough to cold and flu season to do me some favors.

I had taken out my remaining contact lens and dug my glasses out of my purse. I could read without them, but some of the small print on the medications made me squint if I tried reading them with my naked eye, so I had located my black-framed librarian specs, let the chicken out to run around, and started checking my pile of medicines against my books. The results were promising. Some were broad-spectrum antibiotics like amoxicillin, prescribed for many specific conditions but also as sort of a preventative in cases like oral surgery or skin infections, where the likelihood of exposure to new ways of getting sick would be high. I decided that Vet and I were both getting a round of those.

A lot of the other bottles I had were full of little white pain pills. I thought about taking some of these for my foot, but I remembered the last time I'd had a teeth out, I got Vicodin or something similar, and had been completely useless and unable to finish a thought for days. Now was probably not the time for a pharmaceutical brain vacation. I saved them for later and took some aspirin instead.

Some of the other medications were of no determinable use, such as blood pressure meds and SSRIs, and others were completely unidentifiable. I chucked the decidedly useless ones onto the lawn.

I gave Vet and I our first doses of amoxicillin and set about working on my foot for travel. The improvised bandages were going to have to do, but I could at least wash the blood out of them. When I unwrapped it, I did my best not to look at my own toes, but emptied a bottle of water over them and dried them on yet another shirt. After this, I would have to start rationing the water. I re-wrapped the foot, then unwrapped it again and redid it more loosely. Good enough.

Vet got more antibiotic cream to the nose and we played the Tongue Game again. After a few tries, he stopped trying to lick his own face and went after mine instead.

I checked him over for any other damage that I could treat, but everything seemed to be scabbing over or getting less swollen on its own. The same could probably be said for my forehead. Still, I took a little more of the antibiotic cream and put it on my eyebrow. No harm in a little additional infection prevention.

My skin felt crispy all over, probably because volcanic ash is not recommended as a dermatological treatment unless you have a doctor who really, really hates you. I didn't think there was much I could do about it, but after some digging I found that I had taken the jar of petroleum jelly with me from the department store. I didn't remember doing it, but it wasn't that surprising. Smashing and grabbing had become default as soon as 'desperate need' mode was switched on. I was just surprised I hadn't tried to stuff that coyote in my backpack, the way I was hoarding everything I came across. The petroleum jelly wasn't a huge relief on my skin, but I figured it might at least protect it from further damage and let it heal a little, so I slathered it all over my exposed parts.

I looked over my books, and there didn't seem to be anything else that I could do. The next piece of advice in the first aid book was that Vet and I should both be taken in for professional medical care. That wasn't going to happen, at least not any time soon. Who knew. Maybe there would be a hospital open in Canada.

Canada was seeming more and more like the Elysian Fields, Nirvana, Valhalla, Avalon. Or home.

Canada seemed like it contained the possibility of home.

CHAPTER SEVEN
POST-APOCALYPSE MODES OF TRANSPORTATION, PART B

In the end, I loaded the moped down with most of the stuff. It would be slow going, but there was no point in traveling fast if I got halfway to the border and starved to death.

The food was diminished, even more so because we had all gorged as part of our healing process, so it all fit in and on the bike. The chicken would have to go in my lap. For one delusional second, I wondered if the chicken would follow me if I rode the moped, but looking into its little black eyes I realized that its tiny brain could not even compute that I was the source of food. I gave it some more parrot seed and put it back in the cage.

There were still a few gallons of gas left in various containers. I topped off the moped's diminutive tank and tied the rest to the handlebars with a leash. The leashes were now strictly for tie-downs. Vet would follow me on his own.

The things left behind included a few tee shirts, the books on well digging, gardening, and cars, all the unnecessary containers that I'd condensed from, and a small pile of odds and ends that I'd hoarded but didn't really need for any reason at all. What was I going to use an apple corer for in a post-apocalyptic wasteland? If I couldn't get that job done with my knife, then I should probably just find some bandits and surrender myself.

I put the chicken on my lap and practiced using only my left foot to balance the moped. It wasn't as hard as I expected. It was heavy, yes, but I could get away with it easily enough and even if I dumped the moped on its side, the worst thing that happened was I fell on the ground. Again, I was happy that I hadn't bought a motorcycle that would have crushed my legs.

Once upon a time, I had seriously considered getting a Honda Rebel instead. Two things stopped me. One, mopeds seemed less complicated and possibly easier to work on myself (should I ever learn anything about the inner workings of motorized vehicles), and two, the only used Honda I found on Craigslist was all the way in California, a trip I didn't have the time or money to take. Also, the idea of driving my first motorcycle all the way back to Portland on I-5 scared the shit out of me.

Once upon a time, I closed the ad for a motorcycle on my laptop and shuffled my phone out of my pajama pile to call about a moped listing instead. The guy on the other end was nice. I changed out of my yoga pants, went out to meet him, and bought his moped with a check. He was only two neighborhoods away, so there was no highway between us. I was glad. I-5 can be brutal.

Of course, I-5 was nothing compared to the highway I was looking at now. Downed trees are hazard enough, but Route 97 was also strewn with downed houses. As I overtook the first few cautious miles, I found power lines and tire blow-outs everywhere. When I encountered a giant lump of lava bomb cooling in the middle of my lane, I left the road entirely to speed around and away from it as fast as I could go.

I could feel the heat coming off of it as I passed. Something about the lava bomb was unsettling, and I kept picturing it even as I left it behind. It was mostly round, aerodynamic, but it had a sharp, hardened stone tail. Like a comet from the earth. In my imagination, it was hollow, and death lived inside. Death could come out of it at any time. Vet made this impression much worse by barking at it as we passed. I goosed the moped back onto the highway on the other side of the bomb and used everything that poor tiny motor had to get away.

I started seeing an increasing number of dead animals. A few had been hit by cars, but many of the birds seemed to have just taken one look at the volcanic sky, said, "Fuck it," and opted out by falling to earth.

There were frogs and lizards dried into crunchy sticks beside the road. Vet tried to eat one, and I had to stop, run, and grab his nose to keep him from swallowing a large ash-covered salamander. Denied the chance to eat it, he peed on it instead. For dogs, there are only so many ways to react to things in life. I wondered how I could show him that pissing on foreign objects was better than eating them. After a moment's consideration, I peed on it too, thinking maybe Vet would get the idea. It probably wasn't an approved method of dog training, but when it came to inter-species communication, he and I were just going to have to muddle along. This was my best shot.

Vet peed on it again for good measure.

The lizard-stick floated away off the shoulder of the road.

I wondered what the hell had become of my life.

Eventually, we passed through another town. There had been nothing but dead fields for miles. Coming up on the first few houses, I wondered if Moro was going to be like the last divot of rust we had passed through, but things here were cleaner, newer, and if possible, even more evacuated-looking. There were no cars left behind. There was a small park, and part of me longed to go set up a new desk-camp and never leave it again, but I knew it wasn't feasible. This was still a coastal state, and the tectonic plates were out to get me. I had to keep running. Volcanoes can catch up to a girl in a hurry.

I let the chicken run around in the park, throwing some more food and water down, and Vet and I hurried off to go through our usual raiding routine. My crowbar was starting to get dented and dirty. Somewhere along the line, it had become my favorite material possession, the strange successor to years of favorite toys and perfectly fitted jeans. I felt like I should be taking better care of it. The gardening book had had a section on tool maintenance, and while I'd only skimmed it, I remembered that sharp instruments could be further sharpened with a rasp and metal tools should be wiped down and then rubbed with motor oil. I remembered that linseed oil was good for wooden handles, too, but my crowbar needed no such fancy shit. I found some motor oil in a garage and lovingly ran a rag over my new favorite toy.

Vet came around the corner, proudly bearing an orange cat in his mouth. It was alive. It was still in the 'alarmed' phase when I saw it, wide-eyed and motionless, but in a minute it was going to cross over into 'angry.' Vet and I were both injured enough as it was without contending with an angry cat. I patted my leg and called Vet over to me. When he got close, I saw the cat preparing to take a swipe at me, so I grabbed it by the showing scruff, and when Vet let it go, I launched it ten feet into the street.

I know, I know. But the cat was fine.

I had to grab Vet before he could chase it down again, because he seemed to think we were playing catch with a live, furry, four-legged frisbee. I held his collar and gave him some jerky out of my bag. The cat wandered off, making sure we knew it wasn't in a hurry or anything.

I took only the best stuff from the houses, including some light fishing gear and butcher's twine. Then we moved on.

We had just passed the Wasco Cemetery when an earthquake hit. I pulled into the middle of the road and stopped, but it was just a small one. I rolled my eyes at it, like an earthquake was an inconvenient red light that just needs to go green already. I danced impatiently on the ball of my good foot, bouncing the moped even more, wiggling in my seat and muttering “Come on, come on” under my breath. Earthquake. Big deal. The ash shifted on the ground.

It stopped. Vet came up beside me. I thought he was just going to beg for attention or more jerky, but his ears were flat on his head and his tail was tucked under his body. His posture suggested that he expected something very bad to happen to him very soon.

Every bird for miles, just settling down after the quake, took off again and went winging north.

I looked down the ash-dusted expanse of the highway. There were hills a little way off. For the first time, I realized what it actually was: A road built in a natural crack in the earth. The god damn thing was a perforated line in the geologically active land.

By looking at Vet, I guessed I had less than a minute

before he put his belly on the ground and froze up on me. I had to make a decision.

I shot away north, into the middle of a giant field, and when I got somewhere that looked flat and safe, I laid down the moped, the dog, and myself in the lifeless furrows, where we could wait to see if the earth would swallow us whole.

There comes a time when the human brain cannot cope. Losing everything and everyone you've ever known, nearly being killed by a volcano, living in a constant state of fear that you have no idea what you're doing, wrecking yourself royally in a car crash . . . these are all things that can put a great strain on the functions of those three pounds of grey neuro-junk we keep between our ears.

Having it bounced violently against the ground by the planet for several minutes does not help.

Repeating that process several times over the course of an afternoon doesn't help, either.

We lay in that field for hours. Each time getting up and going seemed possible, another tremor would start. Most of them were minor, but there is no way of knowing when an earthquake starts how extreme it's going to get. So we stayed, and I started hallucinating.

The first hallucination seemed so reasonable that I didn't think anything was strange. I just thought that there was no earthquake. The shaking, the bouncing eyeballs, the noise . . . it all started to seem like a perfectly normal thing that people sometimes experience, like tunnel vision from standing up too fast, or limb weakness from physical exhaustion. Suddenly it was so clear. I had just been overdoing it. This wasn't a major planetary event in a chain of events that was destroying all remains of civilization as I had known it. This was just a thing that happens sometimes. It would pass in a minute. Possibly I should think about taking some over-the-counter drug to remedy the feeling. *Yeah,* I thought. *I should take a couple ibuprofen or something. Don't want to go around having earthquakes all day.*

In reality, my head was jittering around on the ground and my body was no longer working. My poor brain was getting rattled around in its case. I was losing hit points by the second. If I could have seen myself, comatose and shaking, I might have been scared, but I wasn't taking part in that reality anymore.

Is it ibuprofen you're supposed to take for earthquakes? Maybe Midol would be better. But I should drink some water because of all that caffeine.

Vet was howling uncontrollably. It was loud, but I processed it as just another annoying feature of getting a bad case of earthquakes.

Maybe I should take three instead of two. This seems pretty bad.

The earthquake stopped. I lay still, drifting in and out. Eventually I pulled my scarf off to use as a pillow, rolled over, and tried to sleep. It didn't work.

Damn. I knew I shouldn't have taken that Midol. Now I'll never get to sleep. Fucking caffeine. I don't even think it worked.

At the time, I wasn't aware of it, but nothing was working at all. I was broken.

The quakes stopped completely after a few hours, but by then my brain was good and bruised. It would take me another two days of stumbling through the basic needs before I had a coherent thought.

I'm not sure if I really slept or not for most of that time. I remember that I would move around and hit my foot on things, and that the pain annoyed me. I did eat and drink. I even fed and watered the animals. The chicken cage latch was too complicated to close up again, so the bird roamed free while I poked uselessly at the cage. Leaning against the moped and staring at the chicken entertained me. For a while, I may have thought I *was* the chicken. When a person is as screwed up as I was, many facets of reality become questionable.

Vet drifted in and out of my perception. I think every time I noticed him, I fed him. It's surprising that he didn't get fat. On the other hand, feeding Vet may have been what kept me feeding myself. *What's this? A dog. Feed it. What's this in my hand? Food. Eat it. I have hands. Maybe I am not the chicken.*

I became very restless, thrashing around trying to get comfortable and pacing across the empty corn field. Sometimes I would fall down in a furrow and just lay there until Vet came and nosed me.

At some point, I thought there were people – not specific individuals, just people –walking around in the field like it was a busy city park. I never saw them, but I knew they were there.

The sun rose and set. This gave me no sense of time. I thought that sunrise and sunset were things that could happen whenever they felt like it.

I know that I slept for a long time on the second or third day, and woke up having done some minor brain healing, because I woke up one sunrise and thought, *What the fuck? I am NOT a chicken. Were those people real? Did I just feed the dog every fifteen god damn minutes? What's wrong with me?*

And suddenly, I was . . . pissed off. Pissed off in a way I had never been before. I felt cold. How DARE the world do this to me? Throwing me out of my house, shaking my brain around, sending volcanoes after me, breaking my foot, forcing me to take medications that may or may not be fucking me up even worse . . . How dare the world touch me? I was going to Canada. Nothing was going to stop me. The world should burn itself to a crisp, and leave me the fuck alone.

Never in my life had I felt rage. It is not a pleasant feeling, but it is certainly not without its uses. I forced my body to work. My marionette muscles scraped themselves off the ground and started packing up. I was going to Canada if it killed me . . . but it wouldn't. It wouldn't dare.

Route 97 was gone, but I found China Hollow Road and kept heading north. Where the road was destroyed, I drove through the fields. Where the road turned away, I plowed on north, refusing to take so much as a minor detour. Vet kept up, but he was working hard for it. Everything ached. I refused to listen to my body. It would heal or it wouldn't. I hardly even cared that I *had* a body. The fundamental bit behind my eyes that was *me* was going nonstop express to the border, with or without a fucking body.

We came to the river.

The river was . . . huge.

Stealing a boat turned out to be just as easy as stealing a car. I didn't expect much from it. I knew exactly nothing about boats, but I thought running any kind of motor in occasional ashfall, over water so disgusting, was probably a short-term solution. Still, I piled everything into a sleek little tech-laden power boat and started looking over the controls. I wedged the chicken into a corner on the floor. Vet followed me into the boat on his own, though it wasn't the most graceful jump I'd ever seen. My moped fit on the back, and was easy to strap down.

I ran my rough hands over the glossy steering wheel.

Every detail of the boat declared it a rich person's toy. It was about thirty feet long, new and clean. Every part was white or chrome. The displays were complicated but the controls were simple.

When I untied it from the dock, I realized that I was now a pirate. That was okay.

The throttle took more force than I'd expected. When I finally got it to go, the boat flew towards the other bank. I was more than halfway to the bushes on the other side before I yelled "Shit!" and started to correct it. My wake watered the plants on the far bank as I aimed the boat upriver. Time for some experimentation.

I spent a few minutes shuffling back and forth on the water, discovering that I could pull the throttle back quickly and then put it in neutral to get the boat to stop. If I throttled it all the way forward, the boat would start skipping over the water. This seemed dangerous. I decided not to do it anymore.

After a few more minutes getting the feel of it, I changed my mind and flew away up the river at full throttle. If I crashed, I crashed. I would be fine. It was only water.

Vet stuck his paws up on the dash and grinned. He seemed to feel the same way.

We made a lot of easy miles that day. Piloting a motor boat is not really difficult. I was still woozy, and my foot was killing me, but there was a comfy chair to sit it and steering the boat was like being the only car on an eight-lane highway. The river was forgiving about the lines I had to stay between. I drank a Vitamin Water and ate a whole meal's worth of food during a long straight stretch. Vet went to sleep in the bottom of the boat. Periodically we would come across other boats, and I would take whatever fuel they had in containers on board. It was a wobbly process getting in and out of them, with my head still spinning and my foot throbbing, but I managed. I even found a few gas cans on a dock. Teetering my way on and off the boat was a simple skill like any other: Acquired by repetition and committed to muscle memory.

We passed through Kennewick that afternoon. I thought about stopping to look for supplies, or even people, but I had as much as I could carry and I didn't manage to resolve my mixed feelings about finding other people until I was already passing the city. I did look around, just in case. I craned my neck around to look back at the city, and, getting lost in my thoughts, forgot to steer, which caused me to scrape the side of a free-floating cargo ship. I screamed and wrenched the steering wheel over, almost flipping the boat.

It's a good thing there wasn't anything else to run into, because even as I tore away from it, I was staring up that massive moving wall of iron, my face squished into the back of my leather seat. Finally I came to my senses and laid off the throttle.

The cargo ship was sinking. I didn't see anyone on board. It was drifting slowly down the river, tilted like it was trying to sit up. There were small holes in the hull. Something way up on the deck was burning and giving off thick, dark smoke. The whole thing had clearly been too close to a volcano and gotten nicked by projectile lava. As it plowed slowly down the river, it created a wake of mud. There was a chemical smell in the air.

Being this close to a sinking ship seemed like bad luck. I moved on.

We passed more scraps of civilization, and then a great deal of green and grey farmland. At Priest Rapids, we came to a dam. I planned to cross to the other side and try to find another boat, but when I ran the current one up onto the shore and walked to the parking lot overlooking the dam, I found that the river had been taken over by the nearest volcano. New rock occupied most of the riverbed. It was already cooled to a thick, hard shell on the outside. Not too far in the distance, there was a mountain goat standing on it. For now, the river was out.

I returned to the boat for my things. Getting the moped off the boat took me nearly an hour, because I had run pretty high aground and had to remove it without crushing myself. There were lots of breaks to drink water and coddle my foot. Vet cuddled me and tried to make me feel better by head-butting all my available body parts. I stopped him before he could bash his face into my broken bone. Then I propped myself back up and gave the moped a final, forceful shove, hoping it would skitter off the other side of the boat. It did.

The moped, as of that moment, was not in any better shape than I was. It no longer had mirrors. The tires were getting low. The smallest of its compartments had taken a good thump and was closed forever. Still, it started on the third try, and it got me all the way to I-90 with minimal trouble, detours included. There was a rough patch where the road and the river both ran between steep hills. Vet ran over the hill. I squeaked the moped through. The muffled, uneven chugging of the engine echoed off the sides.

When we found the place where the road turned into I-90, Vet and I took a break to drink some water and pee on things. We weren't far enough from the Cascade chain to say that the land was really hospitable, but things on the ground were starting to clear up. I could see a thunderstorm headed our way, and thought it might be for the best. We could use a good shower. So could the whole damn world. Still, I packed back up and got going quickly, trying to run east ahead of the storm.

By the time the rain caught us, we were on the edges of Spokane. The last few miles weren't easy. The road was covered in totaled cars, sometimes containing things I could have done without seeing. Evacuation must have happened here, too, so far from the Cascades. I wondered why. Then I looked south.

A great gaping crack in the earth was venting steam. It didn't come up to city limits, but if I paid attention, I could feel it in the air. The entire Spokane metro area was becoming sweat lodge.

Was it safe in the city? There was no way of knowing, but it was probably as safe as anywhere else on this stupid planet. Time to resupply and reconsider.

Getting into the actual city was made more difficult by the destruction of bridges and overpasses, but I bumped my way over some medians and got in anyway. Being surrounded by buildings was surreal after so many miles of fields and forest. I puttered by an insurance company and laughed. So much for that shit, right?

I parked my poor moped and looked around. There were still a good number of cars, but no people that I could see. Fliers were stuck to lamp posts and signs in a strangely uniform way. I brushed one off to read it.

EVACUATION NOTICE

All residents of ***Spokane Metro Area***

are to be evacuated

From ***Spokane International Airport.***

Please do not attempt other evacuation routes.

All other routes from Spokane are hazardous.

Measures are being taken to ensure your safety.

Passenger planes will begin taking civilians to safety starting at ***5:00 PM.***

Planes will run until all evacuees has been safely removed from . . .

The message was much longer than it needed to be, crowding the safety-orange paper with black ink. All the damn thing really had to say was, "Go to the Airport. Run." It explained all the accidents on the roads west of town.

They had all followed directions. The streets were empty. I wondered if there had really been any safe place to land. Maybe they were still up there, circling the earth. Maybe they made an emergency landing in the ocean. Whatever happened to them, an entire city's worth of people had left their stuff behind for me.

I stole another vehicle from a downtown dealership. This time it was a van, which was wonderful. There was room to lay down and put my foot up. I rolled my poor moped right in the sliding side door. It had a tape player and I had rescued some of the audio tapes from the other car, so I got to hear music again. Out of curiosity, I pushed the FM button with my gross dusty finger and scanned the stations.

Recording.

Nothing.

Nothing.

Recording.

Nothing.

Oh, well.

Being in the van was so nice, like having a miniature apartment, that I didn't even mind the meandering I had to do trying to figure out how to point it towards Canada.

Vet and I went through the raiding-a-city routine and headed out. I drove with my left foot. Successfully.

With some weaving and guessing, and a lot of squinting at signs that were obscured by ash and steam, we resumed our trip north. I ran the air conditioning until the engine started to choke. The flier turned out to be right. Trying to evacuate north was hazardous.

Just when I was getting used to the van, I had to give it up.

I had taken the Spokane Falls Boulevard Bridge, which was still standing and only minimally cluttered, and wound my somewhat confused way north to the edge of the city. I passed an airport, and briefly thought about trying to steal a plane, but sometimes facts just have to be faced: I was lucky I figured out how to pilot the boat. When I pictured myself trying to fly an airplane, I just knew that it wasn't going to go well. I would kill myself, possibly without even leaving the ground first. Also, I doubted that planes were the kind of thing where people just left a key laying around that magically started them up. Airplanes have dials and knobs and important meters and shit. Even if it worked, flying in a hunk of metal thousands of feet above the ground is not the time to be unsure. I looked away from the airport and put it out of my mind.

The farther I got from Spokane, the less the landscape resembled the world I was used to. Mordor is really awesome when you're watching it in a movie theater. Not so much when it's right in front of you.

Finally, I hit a lava flow going right across the highway. I hadn't even known that there was a Mount Spokane, but there was, and the thing had popped like a planetary zit. How the hell was I supposed to get across a lava flow? I backed the van far away from the bubbling, sulfurous mass and started looking through my geology book. How long does it take a fat snake of lava to cool?

Spoiler: The bottom layers of a thick lava flow do not cool for years. Years.

I laid on the horn, trying to do any small thing that might express my rage. What the fuck was I supposed to do now? Steal a hot air balloon?

Yes.

I backtracked into Spokane and broke into some more houses until I found a phone book. And this next part, it is quite possible that no one will believe. I had to spend a few minutes deciding whether or not I believed it myself.

In Spokane Valley, there is a company that manufactures, sells, and rents hot air balloons.

Ludicrous.

When I got there, I parked next to a van twice the size of mine in the parking lot. On the side, it advertised for balloon rental. And it contained a hot air balloon rig. And of all fucking things, the *keys* were in it. Rather than second-guess my luck, I promptly transferred everything from my van, stole the new one, and drove the hours back to where the lava had gotten in my way. The van was heavy. The keys jingled when I hit bumps. The jingling was slightly dampened by a rubber hot air balloon on the key ring, red and yellow and blue.

I spent the next several days trying to figure out how to unpack and set up a hot air balloon, injuring myself quite often and trying to attach hoses to things with a baffled look on my face that most closely resembled a baboon trying to assemble a high-end gaming computer from scratch.

My stash of water was dwindling. Vet was needy.

Even the chicken was restless. But this was the only way I could think of to cross the lava without going hundreds of miles out of my way, so I kept working on it. The truck that transported the balloon had some pamphlets on their construction and operation, the kind of low-quality information that usually gets handed out to tourists, but still useful in its way. For instance, I learned that the way to start getting the damn thing up in the air is to lay it out on the ground and blow a fan into it until it was mostly inflated. The balloon truck was prepared for this, and contained not only a fan, but a power source for it. Once the balloon is mostly full of air, you start heating it, and the balloon starts to point upward instead of laying on the ground like a condom for an ice giant. During this entire process, I lived in mortal terror of setting the balloon on fire.

I surprise myself sometimes. I'll spend days trying to accomplish something, feeling like a total idiot, and then, as soon as said thing is accomplished, I just know that *I am a fucking genius* and wouldn't admit that I had ever thought otherwise.

This balloon thing was actually going to work.

The downside was that, once again, I couldn't take everything with me. My moped was going to be a casualty, which was the most upsetting thing. I walked it off the road and covered it with the tarp. Just in case I could come back for it some day.

Most other things I managed to squish into my frame-pack. I put my last few water bottles into an outside pocket and wished I had found more. Crystal-clear burbling streams were not exactly in abundance here in Mordor.

When I had almost finished packing, I found myself giving the chicken sidelong glances. It hadn't laid any eggs in days. I was running low on parrot food. The chicken had spent a lot of time running around scratching in the ash but still seemed to be doing generally okay. Taking it with me seemed to be getting dumber and dumber. I couldn't bring myself to kill it for food. The time was probably coming to leave it behind. *Still,* I thought, *why not take it on one last ride?* This chicken could break the flying record for its kind.

I held on tight to the chicken and got into the balloon. Vet jumped in. I untied the ropes, and after some ground-skimming and screaming, we flew.

The elementary aspects of 'piloting' a hot air balloon are easy. There is a burner, and one controls the propane it burns to heat up the air in the balloon. I made the balloon go up.

Once the balloon is up, it takes years of training to have any remote semblance of control over what direction it goes. I did not have this training, and for quite some time I didn't even realize that I needed it. I was in a big basket, with a dog, a backpack, and a chicken, entirely focused on keeping myself well above some still-burning lava. I had to give it a lot of gas because the air here was already bordering on hot and the balloon didn't want to stay up. Vet wasn't happy that I was ignoring him in my efforts to keep us in the air. He grumbled and spun in circles, rocking the basket.

The balloon drifted right over the lava flow. The hot Mordor-ish air became a cool breeze on the other side. Toxic smells that I hadn't even noticed I was inhaling started to dissipate. Since I had superheated the balloon to get it over the warm air pocket, it shot up a hundred feet when it hit the cooler atmosphere. My eyes almost bugged out of my head with fear that I was going all the way to outer space. I cut the propane down to almost nothing.

I started experimenting with the balloon. There were two different inputs for the burner. According to the touristy pamphlets, one was for propane gas (loud and hot) and one was for liquid propane (quieter and cooler). Playing around with them, teaching myself to fly a hot air balloon, was kind of fun.

While I was busy with that, the wind started taking me west.

Vet shuffled himself around on the floor of the basket, trying to find the position where the wind ruffled his fur the least. My own currently short hair was making a valiant effort to blow straight up my nose, catching in my eyelashes and poking into my ears. When I could get my hair to stay out of the way, though, the view was spectacular. I was floating over hell in a balloon basket, but it was a lot better than walking in it. Ash started to look like snow. I could pretend that all the little houses were intact and had people in them. The muscles in my back started to relax for the first time in weeks. Everything was okay from up here. The landscape was pretty shitty when you had to live in it, but going over it was more like an exotic vacation. I thought about places I would like to go hot air ballooning over. Was Yellowstone still a place? Probably not. Probably it was now either one giant pit or one giant volcano. Possibly both. Too bad I never got to see it. Maybe the Grand Canyon was still a thing.

Up above the apocalypse, things were almost serene.

At least, until the wind started taking me west, back towards the Cascades. The balloon would never make it all the way back to the mountains, but my main goal in life was to get as far away from the Pacific Rim as possible and here was mother nature taking me straight back there.

What a bitch.

I decided to bring the balloon down before I could get any farther off track.

There's a way to let hot air out of the balloon by pulling a rope and affecting a little flap at the top. This should be done gradually, in short bursts, as a carefully controlled process. I did not know this, so when I discovered that flap, I let most of the heat out at once and started plummeting to earth.

No amount of propane was going to get me back up in time. We did a small temperature-change jig while making inexorable progress toward a crash landing. The swinging basket knocked over a few weedy saplings and then landed, with a gritty splash, in Loon Lake, which may have been exactly where we belonged. Vet and I floundered. The chicken, to my total disbelief, swam away.

Vet chugged around in circles for a minute, then started putting some distance between himself and the sinking basket. I wallowed around trying to rescue my bag and follow him. He made it to shore first. I bopped myself on the head with my frame-pack repeatedly, trying to haul it to the little man-made beach. At one point I had to doggie-paddle around a sunken boat. Anything in this area that was not a natural land formation was trash.

I flopped up on the beach.

Vet stepped on me.

The chicken was nowhere to be seen.

CHAPTER EIGHT
SELF DEFENSE: THE BANDIT PALACE

We walked for five or six hours before we found a place that was still identifiable as a remnant of civilization. Loon Lake hadn't been much help. The whole of the lakefront property had been shaken to death. The only useful thing Loon Lake had given us was a canoe paddle that I cut down to use as a crutch. My foot was not improving with any great speed. Not really surprising, considering what I was putting it through.

My hobbling skills, on the other hand, were growing by leaps and bounds.

Frequent breaks made traveling a gratifying if challenging task. Every yard gave me some satisfaction. No one could have known it from the way I behaved. I yelled at trees. I whined a lot. I tried to figure out a way to strap my frame-pack to Vet. Dogs cannot wear human backpacks, no matter what stupid thing you try, but I did manage to rig a sort of old-school donkey-pack for him with rope and plastic bags, which he completely ignored.

This was the best possible result. He could have chewed it off, or spun in circles trying to get a look at it, or scraped it off on a tree. Instead, he just forgot about it, and when we got going again he trotted along without the least complaint. In that moment, I loved that dog more than anything or anyone ever. He had taken thirty pounds off my back, just done it, like saving my sorry ass was the most natural thing in the world and his whole god damn mission in life. We still took a lot of breaks after that, but my body was no longer in a constant state of emergency.

Every muscle was sore, but the pain seemed to be cyclical: Destroy old, grow new, destroy old, grow new. I was getting stronger even as I was shredding my body to bits.

Picture poor little Mab, holding her pieces together, crutching her way to Canada with her big supply-laden dog and her new anime haircut. Falling leaves, ash, and shreds of the trash that was civilization batter her equally. She is taking lots of breaks to eat peanut butter with her fingers and rest her mangled foot. As she walks, her lips are hidden because of her air-filter scarf, and her determined walk is masked by her crutch . . . but there is a look in her eyes. It says, *World . . . move.*

That night, we made it to Chewelah. I'm not sure I would call it a city, but it was a hell of a lot closer to metro than the miles of fields and trees we had left behind us, and it was mostly still standing. I planned to spend a day or two here. I hadn't felt an earthquake all day, so being indoors for a while was sorely tempting. I thought about trying to find a hotel. It would be nice to have a bedroom, all made up, with four walls and a mattress and the illusion of a normal night out of town. Evacuated houses had a high heebee-jeebee factor, and also contained the risk that they weren't evacuated after all, which meant either dead bodies or potentially dangerous live ones. In the end, though, I got to thinking about the electronic locks on hotel rooms and realized I didn't have the energy. I broke into the nearby hardware store and set up camp in the paint aisle instead.

Now seemed like a good time to cuddle up to my survival book and figure out some things. I tore out the pages that had lists of recommended supplies, sticking them up on paint cans with masking tape in a neat row. Then I dumped out my bag in front of it.

A person can use much more than she can carry.

This is why we have houses.

Well, had. Had houses.

Now it's just me. I used to have a house. Now I have a backpack.

I foraged around the hardware store and others on the block until I had most of the things my survival book recommended. Complete fishing gear. Strong rope. Flashlights and batteries. Waterproof bags. Candles. Fire-starters. Safety pins. Steel water bottle. I even found a gun.

Actually, I found several guns. At first, I thought they were real, but upon more careful examination of the store display I eventually realized that they were pellet guns, good mimics of actual firearms that worked on CO_2 cartridges and shot glorified BBs. Now I was less scared of them. Real guns are scary. These were just toys.

Now, I can say that pellet guns are not toys. They are just as complicated as the real things and even the basic BB ammo can cause some damage. Sometimes, you can find little pointed 'field hunting' ammo, like I did, and then what you have is actually a force to be reckoned with. It won't bring down a bear, but it will bring a squirrel down out of a tree and really wreck someone's day if you shoot him in the nose.

I picked a gun, located compatible ammo by checking boxes and instructions, and made them the last items I added to my new and improved survival kit.

We had spent three days camping in the hardware store. My backpack now represented the combined best of my book learning and common sense. My foot had been itching, which seemed like a sign of healing. It was, too. The bone wasn't knitting together quite the way it should, but it was knitting. Time to move on. I was hoping to do so in style this time around.

There was no car dealership in Chewelah, at least not that I could find. I went back to an RV park I had passed on the way into town. There were a few hulking off-white mobile homes left, but two had flowerbeds where tires should have been and the first promising one I came to had no keys. The second one I broke into had spare keys tucked under the floor mat, but while discovering this, I also became aware that a side window was broken and a number of raccoons had moved in.

The Battle of Raccoon Trailer was brief and mostly bloodless. I opened all the doors and windows, then chased the raccoons around with my oar-crutch until they ran. They made a variety of horrible noises to show their displeasure at being evicted. The last hold-out, a fat one with a scar cutting through the furry bandit-mask on his face, hissed and bit my crutch. I stuck the crutch out the door and shook it until he fell off. Vet ran up and bit him. I thought about intervening, but if Vet was going to start catching his own food, I knew I should let him. He was obviously winning against the raccoon. I closed the RV door. Nature is not pretty sometimes.

The RV was on the smaller end, but it didn't have much gas and I didn't find any more. I drove it left-footed for an hour or so, until the gas gave out. Then Vet and I walked.

That night, we crossed the border into Canada. I almost didn't notice it. If not for the bars across the road, I might have just crawled on north forever. Moving on down the road had become my default state of being. I stopped when I saw the barriers, blinked, and ducked under them without fully understanding their significance. Soon Vet laid down to take a break. I joined him. After a few minutes, my brain finally started dealing with information from my eyes again, and thus I became aware that I was sitting in front of a giant sign.

Welcome to Canada!

Even now, I am grateful to whatever powers may be for that sign. Having made it across the border, I started to feel awake and alive again. I started looking where I was going. Noticing things. Which came in handy a few miles down the road, when we hit the Bandit Palace.

Christina Lake Village was a hotel with a secondary building of shops. There was a large nature mural on the south walls and the words "Welcome to Christina Lake" in whirling cursive script. The main building was painted cartoon-lake blue, cream, and eggplant.

Even from a quarter-mile down Crowsnest Highway, I noticed a few things out of place with it now. Most hotels do not resort to road blocks to get people to stop. They also don't have generators keeping the electricity on after an apocalypse. As I got closer, I could see a bonfire behind the barrier in the street, dancing in the wind and making the lines on the highway shimmer. Someone had hung a sign over it that said "Welcome, Survivors!" There was a whole lot of welcoming going on.

Stopping my body from running towards the light

was only half a battle. The impulse was there, but so was a kind of repulsion. It was a strange new place. There would be people. People who were no longer living in any kind of civilization, people who weren't bound by any law . . . people who might be bigger and stronger and not like me very much. Then I saw them.

Five human shapes came around the corner of the main building and approached the bonfire. They were talking. They seemed drunk. Once I spotted them, the urge to run up and join their party was so strong that resisting was like trying not to breathe. I couldn't understand any of the words they were saying, but content didn't matter to me. The simple fact that communication in my language was going on was the greatest joy. I wanted to run babbling into their midst and cuddle them all into comas. I knew they could be dangerous, but part of me didn't care, and that part was glowing hot.

Neurochemicals raged.

My feet held.

Good god damn thing, too.

I watched them from the woods.

The forest ran along the road on the east side of the highway, so I laid my stuff down and tied Vet to a tree a few yards in. He protested, but at least he limited it to grumbling and pulling against the rope. He had already made several attempts to bolt for the bonfire and the people, but each time I had managed to coax him back. If he tried again, I might have let him go. You can tell a lot about a person by how they treat a dog. On the other hand, a person trying to survive might be really nice to a big useful dog and kill a competing human outright, so the dog test would be totally useless and Vet was staying tied to a tree whether he liked it or not. He could frown at me and make mumphing sounds all he wanted.

I made one attempt at climbing a coniferous tree, but it wasn't an easy or quiet process, so I crawled under the lowest boughs until I was close enough to see and hear the people around the fire. Pitch and needles invaded my privacy. My heart thudded harder and harder until it seemed too big for my body, inflated by the thought *If you can see them, they can see you.*

I laid down, trying to calm my body. I reassured it that no one was going to see an ash-colored girl under a pine tree in the dark, especially if there's a huge, crackling bonfire in the way. My body didn't listen. It was too busy suffering in the conflict between running to my fellow humans and fleeing from the same. I put my face down in the mud and needles, disappearing in the dark. I tried to breathe.

Some details were visible in the night. The hotel was large, and may once have been a pretty sleepy place, but now it looked like a showboat. Strings of white Christmas lights covered the building. Empty liquor bottles were lined up on railings, filled with candles and dead flowers. Benny Goodman played on speakers rigged by the doorways. The words "Come On In" were painted on the doors over big, sloppy smiley faces. The paint, assuming it was paint, was a dark reddish-brown.

Judging from the voices, there were three men and two women around the fire. One man and one woman were loud, authoritative, and laughed without filtering their glee through civility.

Friends. The community-craving base humanity in me was pushing hard. *Friends. Friends friends friends. Go to them. Be saved. Listen. Speak. Be adopted. Call it home and let this fucked-up road trip be over.*

At some early point, ludicrous though it was, I

thought *Maybe there's someone I know.*

I watched this camp all night. Nothing I saw or heard made me any less scared of these strangers, but I was trying hard to think of them as simple merry bandits. Rascals, sure, but good souls deep down. I started creating background stories for them in my head and imagining conversations we could have when I came out of the bushes. We would get drunk together. They would scratch Vet between the ears. A room would be ready for me in the hotel. The combination of fantasy and observation passed the hours.

In the morning, more travelers came north on the Crowsnest Highway, just as I had. The newcomers had a truck. The bed was filled with food, water, gas, clothes, and tools. The leading lady bandit greeted them with enthusiasm, waved them out of the car, and shot them in the face.

In the tradition of living things everywhere, people found their homes destroyed and set out in search of a new one as far away as possible.

A number of them used this highway as a means to try to reach a city that hadn't been destroyed, or just any stable and vacant place on Earth. Everywhere people went, they had to keep looking. That meant that any number of them would eventually end up on this highway.

Christina Lake Village was ideally located for stopping all travelers. There wasn't another major highway for miles. It was in the cup of a valley, on the outskirts of a town, and near a lake that might still have living fish in it. None of the nearby landscape had exploded. There were no neighbors. The entire time I was hiding in the woods, the worst thing that happened to this camp was a thunderstorm, during which Vet and I hid under my last tarp and listened to the rain patter.

It was so good that my desire to be accepted here was starting to temper my desire to avoid risking a shot in the head, and that says something. Fortunately for me, I never let anything win out over my desire to avoid catching a brain-pan bullet. I was going to give this whole place a pass and sneak around.

I went to feed Vet before setting out, and realized that I was down to a few days' worth of food.

My fear of the Bandit Palace had solidified. I could guess how many people they had either absorbed or killed by the superfluous number of vehicles parked in the large hotel lot. That number was high. Any desire to run up and hug them had been taken down by the first shot fired.

Now I had to consider that they had all the supplies I needed, and I might have to steal some. This was not a good plan. Still, in whatever brief periods I had been really hungry, I learned a fear of ever being so again. Sooner or later I was going to have to learn to hunt and gather. If that time came too soon, I might starve before I figured it out.

The more I thought about it, the more sense it made. I should steal some food from the bandits. That would practically make me Robin Hood. I would steal from the assholes, and give to . . . well, me. I was needy. I would be doing the world a favor if these guys starved. Maybe some more peaceful group would take over the Bandit Palace.

Probably not.

But still.

I was going to rob these evildoers blind.

I fed Vet and got out my little pellet gun.

Thinking back on it, I was very lucky that the bandits hadn't set up a patrol to sweep the woods. Less lucky was that I was stupid enough to sweep their camp.

Before I did anything else, I took Vet far north of the camp. I wanted to tie him to a tree again to keep him from doing anything stupid, but I didn't want to hobble him in case something happened while I was gone. He wouldn't sit and stay while I crutched off, so I waited until he wasn't paying attention and meandered away a little at a time. This seemed to work. It was easier on my foot, too.

I went back to my hiding spot under the tree and planned a raid.

There seemed to be ten or twelve people in the camp. Only two of them had guns: the leader types I saw on the first night. There were only a few women, and aside from the gun-toting bandit queen, they skulked around like scullery maids in a medieval storybook. The men were another story. Most showed a certain deference to the gun-wielders, but otherwise acted like they were just trying to get back to their normal day-at-the-office routine. Most of them slept at night. Two or three spent their days working on equipment or constructing better barricades. As far as I could tell, the rest didn't do anything at all. They only came out of the hotel rooms to yell at each other and play cards.

While I was patiently scouting, gathering all possible information to filter down into a plan, the sun went down and it all went wrong.

The Bandit King and Queen started packing up a truck.

In the settling dark, the two were throwing sacks into a truck and talking about where to go next to retrieve more ammunition and canned food. The woman was hefting surprisingly large bags into the bed of the Ford. I could see her silhouette by the bonfire. She had a Bettie Page haircut and a sharp profile. When she turned through the firelight,

I could see blue star tattoos on her arms. The muscles under them changed shape as she lifted another box.

In a weird way, she inspired me. A lifetime of struggling with 'becoming the modern woman,' with feminism and femininity and shaving my armpits but feeling guilty about it, got simplified down very quickly. I've read a million stories about women coming of age, achieving things other than what was expected of them . . . fiction meant to show what women were capable of becoming. The Bandit Queen showed me that there had been just about enough 'becoming' for women. It was time to just 'be,' instead. To rise up and cry, "We get it! We can! Now let's just shut up and *do* already!" The other women slinking around the camp had reverted to the extreme of traditional roles, but the Bandit Queen herself was forging a one-girl post-feminist society.

I decided I was going to live in it, too. I studied her for too long before getting back to my plan, but maybe too long was just long enough to learn.

After sizing up the Queen, I expected the Bandit King to be a rockabilly type with wingtip shoes, but then I got a good look at him. He turned out to be a completely different story. Jumping up on the bed of the truck, he revealed himself in the bonfire glow. His beard belonged on a cartoon hermit, and given another month, may graduate to wizard status. He wore a combination of camouflage and black Kevlar.

My guess was that they hadn't started out together, but came to some kind of accord where they could both be their Alpha Bandit selves. From what they'd accomplished, it looked like they made a hell of a team.

Peeking out from under the pine bough, I think I started to smile. I was probably loopy by this point. Thinking clearly is something that happens indoors, with lots of coffee, and can in no way be achieved while hiding under a sap-dripping tree with an empty stomach and a broken foot. Hours of consideration about the safest way to take only what I needed went straight out the window. I was just going to steal their truck.

Some lessons in life are hard. Here's one: Stealing a car is much harder when it belongs to survivalists with guns.

The Royal Bandits left the truck alone for about thirty seconds. It was running. So was I. Even with my messed-up foot and my wobbly muscles, I ran.

The truck was twenty yards from the tree line. I almost tripped when I first wiggled out from under the pine branch, but I threw down a hand, bounced my palm off the ground, and kept going in a controlled fall until I slammed into the truck. My face hit the side window. The lock tab on the passenger's side door was an inch from my wide-open eye, and it was down.

I tried the handle anyway, yanking on it three times before I started doing a combination of a run and a slide around to the other side of the truck. The headlights lit up my quivering thighs like stars in a post-apocalypse burlesque show.

Somebody yelled, "Hey!"

When I turned, I could see the man who called out. He was very close, but standing still. I brought up my toy gun and shot him in the face. His nose caved in. I looked away.

I fell onto the door handle on the driver's side and yanked. For a second, I thought it was locked, and I was going to get shot, but it gave on the second try and I rocketed into the cab. The door bounced closed behind me. I stuck my right foot across the seat and positioned myself to drive with my left.

The truck stalled.

My left leg flailed around in the footwell. It hit an unexpected pedal.

I looked at the stick shift.

I hadn't driven a vehicle with manual transmission since high school, but I remembered at least one thing: You need two feet to do it. I only had one.

People from the Bandit Palace, discernible only as shadow, started running toward the truck.

I locked the door, closed my eyes, and tried to think back ten years or so.

In high school, I dated a Carhartt-wearing modern greaser type. These are unusual in New York City, but I found one. He owned a car and worked on it himself. Maybe I should have made the effort to learn something about cars while I had him around, but teenage me wasn't too concerned about how engines worked.

This boyfriend, Charlie, had somehow found a whole gang of friends who owned and worked on cars in a city where everyone takes the subway. One of his friends worked as a part-time painter and had a truck, which Charlie borrowed and insisted on teaching me to drive. He thought a girl trying to drive stick would be funny and cute.

I didn't even know how to drive an automatic, or what the difference was. Growing up with a Metro pass can do that to a girl.

I tried. After ten minutes of carefully trying to follow his instructions while he crowded me in the cab, he stopped me and said I should either get it right or give up trying, because the transmission couldn't take it. I had no idea what that meant, but no teenage girl can admit that sort of thing. He rubbed a crunchy flannel sleeve against my arm and tried to be more encouraging than frustrated. Finally, I got the truck out of the parking lot.

We left the city and headed up the Palisades Parkway. Charlie said that if we got pulled over, he would jump into the driver's seat and we would be fine. We made it all the way to Tappan.

I pulled into a gas station and smiled at Charlie. He tousled my hair and made a 'how cute' noise. We went inside. He got a soda and a slice of pizza that had probably been sitting on the wire rack since the dawn of time. We went back out to the truck.

In the space of five minutes, I had completely forgotten how to drive it. I couldn't get us going again. Charlie took over and drove us back to the city.

I never drove stick again.

Until now.

The bandits were only a few feet from the truck and were making a final lunge by the time I brought my right foot around. Blood was dripping in my eyes. I tried to shift and stalled it. A man covered in half-healed wounds appeared beside my window and yanked on the door. For a second, seeing his face, I wondered if this had turned out to be the zombie apocalypse after all.

He slammed his arm into the window. The glass rattled in its track, but didn't break. I surprised myself quite a bit by rolling down the window and palm-heeling him in the nose before he could try again. He fell back. I shut my eyes tight and tried starting the truck again.

The pain in my foot shot all the way up to my thigh. I was wearing my boot again, because the swelling had gone down some and I figured a leather work boot with a lot of socks was as good a cast as any, but I had tied it loosely with twine and may have left my foot too much room to move around in. Still, I got the truck into first gear. I started pulling away from the Bandit Palace at a few pathetic miles an hour. The zombie-man from my window grabbed the side mirror, but it cracked off in his hands and he dropped out of sight. Someone else jumped into the bed of the truck. I ignored him and tried shifting into second. It stalled. I panicked and braked hard. The man in the back of the truck staggered, tripped over a lumpy sack in the dark, and bounced his head off the cab. His face made a loud sound on impact, and I jumped.

I hadn't blinked since getting the truck started. My eyes were starting to get dry and blurry, and the muscles around them were tiring. I swiped blood away from them one more time. Then I made myself close them.

I didn't need to see. I just needed to drive the truck in a straight line.

My good timing was a total fluke, but this time I got it to shift smoothly all the way into
third gear. I was leaving! I felt like one of the birds freed from that pet store. Gone!

A blinding blue-white light filled my remaining mirrors. Cruising steadily away, I chanced my life on a look back. Don't ask me why. It's just something that people do.

The Bandit King and Queen were barely visible next to a large generator-powered work light aimed at my truck. They were both aiming long, dark, gun-shaped somethings at me. I slid down in my seat, almost slipped off the gas, saved it, and drove on.

A shadow came up in my rear view mirror.

There was a round of gunshots.

The shadow disappeared.

I switched out my bad foot, putting the good one on the gas, and bombed down the road.

A few minutes down, I finally had a thought in my head that was not about broken bones or manual transmissions. It was about the number of vehicles I'd seen back at the bandit camp. A glance in the mirror showed that the bandits hadn't started one up to chase me yet. There were no lights. But there was a darker shadow at the bottom of the back window. When I whipped the truck off the main road, the shadow slid to one side. Suddenly I knew what it was, and I was not happy about it.

The secondary road led down to the lake. I pulled the truck all the way out onto the beach to hide it behind a camp house, then shut off everything. I snooped around to see what goodies the bandits left in the truck.

There was a handgun, a pair of binoculars, and a Maglite in the glove box. There was a walkie-talkie on the seat, but I was afraid of somehow butt-dialing the bandits with it so I rolled down a window and threw it into the lake.

I used the Maglite to look over the gun. It was heavy, probably loaded, and had moving parts. The real deal. I held it far in front of me and kept the business end pointed out the open window.

Despite my shaky hands, I played with it a little. Flicked the safety on and off. Looked down the barrel with its little tiny sight on the end. Ran a finger over the bumpy waffle-textured parts. I didn't want to mess with it too much because I had always been quite sure that, if you put me in the same room with a gun for more than a few seconds, it was inevitable that I would shoot myself in the foot.

Absolutely the last thing I needed to do right now.

Not only was I trying to work with a foot and a half, but the night was quiet, gunshots were loud, and the sound would probably draw the bandits to me.

Speaking of bandits.

I thought I knew what the dark shape in the window had been, and when I got out of the truck and opened the tailgate, I was proven right. The man who jumped into the bed of the truck had stood up just as the Queen started shooting at me, and he was hit instead. He was lying dead under the window. Before dying, he bled all over the supplies. Stickiness I could deal with. Bodies were new to me. I couldn't kill a chicken for food. Dealing with a dead human being was just not one of my life goals, but here it was, at the top of my to-do list:

Remove corpse from truck.

I squared my shoulders, tucked my chin, and decided that this couldn't be any worse than what I had already been through. He's just meat, and he needs to be somewhere else. Spring cleaning for my new truck. I rubbed my hands together and grabbed his leg.

He was too cold to be a living person, but not cold enough to just be a thing. There was no tension to the flesh. My hands contracted automatically, like if they squeezed him harder they would detect some sign of life and this would not be happening. I tried to follow through with my plan but my muscles wouldn't do it. I sprang back and threw up in a nearby canoe instead.

While I was recovering, shaking on my hands and knees on the beach, I invented good reasons that I had to do this and do it now. People were after me. I couldn't leave him in there to rot. I might get sick. He might bloat and explode. I needed the supplies he was laying on. It would be easier to do now, in the dark, than in the morning when I had to really look at him.

I thought about touching him again, and considered abandoning the truck.

No. I wanted the truck.

My face started to move muscles on its own. My expression became one that I had worn often enough in my life that my friends had a name for it. All on its own, my 'beaten and sick' face was becoming my well-known "Fuck you, I can do it myself" face. The one that said I will open this pickle jar if it kills me and any offer of help will be met with a dill to the ear hole. The expression most often given to friends trying to get me to go to the doctor and fuckhead boyfriends who try to teach me things I already know.

A few months ago, a dead body in a truck would have been an occasion for intensive therapy sessions. I knew this. I made an effort not to revert to that P.S. thinking. Now a dead body was just something I needed to handle, but instinctual revulsion was causing trouble.

I never did overcome the revulsion. Instead, I got smart and tied a rope around his legs so I didn't have to touch him. Then I hauled him out of the truck bed. The noise his body made when he hit the ground still sounded like a human taking a hard thump, and I had to stop myself from asking if he was okay. Of course he wasn't okay. He was dead.

I found another canoe, hauled him into it, and pushed it off into the lake. He may have been a bandit, but I couldn't just leave him on the beach to get eaten and rot. Doing the best we can in the worst we face is what makes us human.

I put it out of my mind and drove away.

If the rest of the bandits came after me, I never saw

them. I took a side road and pulled off down a long driveway half-hidden by the trees. The house at the end was a charred husk, but there was a shed still standing and it was big enough to pull the truck into.

Ladders hung from the ceiling. Garden tools and snow shovels were neatly arranged on wall hooks, red and blue and green, polished wood grain and oiled metal, looking like suburban civilization and smelling like cut grass.

I spent a full day there: Reading, eating, re-bandaging, and healing. My books kept the bandits, both living and dead, out of my mind. When I started reading, I was in the section of the book about trapping and skinning, but to keep from thinking about the dead bandit I moved on to a section about edible plants. By nightfall, I was learning to cook with minimal supplies and gather water from trees using plastic bags. I fell asleep early.

Hidden away down a private drive in the Canadian near-wilderness, I found some peace. I slept for twelve hours or more, waking only for a minute every few hours to shake off the dreams and cycle some water through myself. The sleep was healing. When I finally got up again, my foot itched but hardly hurt and my mind was clear. Optimism started sneaking in unnoticed. I stretched out my joints.

The sun was up. I was fed and not in much pain. I had a truck and food and a lot of highway in front of me.

Now I just had to find my damn dog.

It was still early, but I drove with the headlights off in case the bandits were looking for their missing truck. I found a hill northeast of the camp. The binoculars from the glove box were scratched, but powerful, and I scanned the bit of Christina Lake visible to me from the far side of the hill. I wanted to try from the very top, but I knew the bandits probably had more than one set of binoculars and I didn't want them to spot me.

Nothing much moved below me. When I saw something that did and focused in on it, it usually turned out to be a bird. Probably some expert tracker somewhere could have picked out broken branches and game trails and located a dog from five miles away based on some bent grass and a nearly imperceptible piece of dog shit, but I saw a whole lot of nothing. My good mood was disintegrating. This was impossible. Vet was gone forever.

I sat behind the wheel of the truck and cried. It was all my fault. I bailed on my faithful canine companion. I should have stormed the Bandit Palace with him and let him attack them by my side, firing my little pellet gun while he tore out their throats.

It would have been a bad plan. He probably would have licked them, wagging his stupid tail, and they would have shot me, but at that moment it seemed like a better outcome than this . . . lost in Canada without my only friend in the whole world.

I got angry with myself. *This is pointless. No sense in sitting here doing nothing.* Still crying, I put some gas from the back into the truck and started to drive away.

A few miles north, I had to stop because caribou were crossing the highway. I slowed down when I saw the first one, then gave up and killed the engine when I saw that a whole herd of them were crossing my path. They were large, healthy-looking animals with hooves the size of my head. Their fur coats were shaggy and varicolored. In a way, they were beautiful. I'd never seen one before.

Most of them ran by in matching strong and graceful gaits. When the herd started to thin out, the last few to cross the highway were less coordinated. They bucked, kicked, and skittered on the pavement, but they made it across the road. Almost as soon as they were gone, a different shape shot out of the trees and bounced over the rumble strip, chasing them with a frantically wagging tail and face of pure joy. I jumped out of the truck.

"VET!"

He fell all over himself trying to change direction, bounced off a few trees, and came to a stop by head-butting my leg. His tongue was lolling so far out I could have tied it in a knot. He was shaking and smiling. I rolled my eyes even while they were watering with happiness and relief. My throat was tight.

"Get in the truck, you stupid dog."

He did.

We mauled each other with affection and ate some celebratory jerky before taking off again. I sang. Vet mumbled and howled and grinned. This was a kind of happiness I had never felt before the apocalypse, and on some level it was strange, but that was perfectly all right.

CHAPTER NINE
POST-APOCALYPSE MODES OF TRANSPORTATION, PART C

The truck lasted for almost a hundred kilometers.

I don't know what that is in miles, but I was watching the remaining signs by the road pretty closely, and that's my best guess. About a hundred kilometers. It was a long way.

Vet and I had some good times in that truck. I washed the bandit blood off when we found a smaller lake, and the truck bed was actually quite comfortable to hang out in. At night, I drew a tarp over it and got to sleep with my legs stretched out. Maybe it was the improved sleep, or maybe just the fact that my adrenal gland finally took a vacation and stop beating on the rest of my body, but I started to feel physically normal again. I took a lot of ibuprofen, drank a lot of water, and took up yoga in the mornings. When I jumped out of the truck bed to stretch one day, I examined myself for signs of healing and found a lot of surprises. My foot looked like a watercolor painting instead of a horror movie prop: Too blue, purple, and yellow, but clean and human. Various cuts and bruises were so improved I had to look closely to see where they had been. On top of all that, I was one fit bitch.

I had always been an acceptable amount of chubby on top of a bone structure equal to that of any two supermodels. Now I had added muscle and all the little pudgy bits had vanished. I still had a thick frame, but everything attached to those big bones went and got amazing. Wide hips were supported by pony-strong legs. To my complete disbelief, not only did I have abs, but I could see them. I poked them several times to make sure they were real. I was never really in bad shape, I was never weak, but somewhere between the end of the world and the Crowsnest Highway, I had evolved into an Amazon warrior. This was surprising to me, but also awesome.

That day, I took the time to sort through the bandit supplies from the truck. Most things were just duplicates of tools and food from my own bag, but there was a treasure chest at the bottom. It looked like a fireproof safe box. The crowbar made short work of the hinges. The box contained whiskey, cigarettes, dark chocolate, two Zippo lighters, salt and pepper shakers, bullets, and a harmonica. It was a post-apocalypse party in a box.

That day, I studied my books and my world. Vet caught and ate a squirrel.

That night, I had a party.

I do not know how to play the harmonica, but I got drunk and did it anyway, and Vet joined me in his own way. We sounded about the same. Finally, I just put down the harmonica and howled with him. We had a grand old time.

Aahooooo!

The next day, a bee flew in the truck window and stung me. I am very, very allergic to bees. The Epi-Pen that I had grabbed on the way out of my apartment saved my life. After I pulled over and stabbed myself with the pen, I lay in the back of the truck to recover and got to thinking that actually, I am not such a totally unprepared dumbass after all.

Normally, this kind of thinking would be followed by some horrible, ego-checking disaster. None came. A few hours later, we got back on the road.

Once, I saw a car in the distance and pulled over, half-burying the truck in the bushes, hiding from this new potential bandit vehicle. I watched it for a full fifteen minutes. It did not get any closer. I got out the binoculars. The car was abandoned and had four flat tires. I got back in the truck and passed it. Instead of feeling foolish for running from an empty car, I gave myself a small nod of approval. There was no reason to be embarrassed for taking precautions. I was doing the right things.

The next day, nothing much happened at all. I stopped long enough to cook a real lunch, and Vet and I ate it on a tarp in the middle of the highway. Any day with spam in it was now a good day.

On our last day with the truck, I started noticing signs of civilization around nine in the morning. Broken-down cars were pulled off the side of the road. When I stopped the truck, I could hear another engine far away. I hobbled up the hill. From the top, I could see the city of Nelson. I backtracked, found another road that headed due north and took it. The bandits were fresh in my mind.

There might have been friendly people in that city, taking in refugees and prepping for the next long winter. But I didn't know, and as long as I had Vet with me, I cared less and less if I ever saw another human being again. I went around.

The truck ran out of gas as I was rounding the northwest side of Slocan Peak.

Then I got out to walk.

I was very practical when it came to what I needed and what I could carry. Vet, on the other hand, wanted to take everything with us.

I was walking away from the truck when Vet came up to me dragging a bag full of spare clothes that I had deliberately left behind. His furry chin was way up in the air to keep the bag from tripping him. He tried to trip me with it instead. It worked. Tripping a girl with one semi-functioning foot is not hard. I recovered well, though.

"What the hell do you think you're doing with that? No. We're leaving it. Drop it. Vet. Drop it. Droooop iiiiit. Vet! Vet, you're so frigging stupid. Vet, drop it. Drop. It."

Eventually I grabbed his nose and made him let go. I put the bag back in the truck.

Vet jumped into the truck and started gnawing on a box.

"Vet. No. Vet! Vet, stop. Come on."

Vet did a playful body flop and rolled around in the bags, tail wagging, head buried under a canvas sack. I put down my backpack. He wiggled his ass at me. Then, by slowly working his bulky body around, he managed to shove just about everything off the tailgate of the truck. He sneezed and jumped down. Looked at the stuff. Looked at me. Looked at the stuff.

There was nothing in there that we really needed, but I sat by and watched as Vet tore it apart. Soon the road was littered with underwear, extra rope, shirts, trash bags, and empty gas cans. A plastic tub full of molding chili exploded when he pounced on it. Finally, Vet started heavily pawing the door of the cab. Still trying to figure out what the hell he was doing, I opened it for him. He jumped in, snuffled around, and jumped back out unsatisfied. I was about to start walking without him, knowing he would catch up, when he broke into a happy pant and stuck his face in one of the sacks. He surfaced with a tube of tennis balls in his mouth, chomping and throwing his head around. He brought it to me. I took it. When I opened the tube, something didn't smell right. Tennis balls should not smell like sulfur. Each ball had a cut in it. When I flexed one, I found out it was full of match heads.

The bandits had made tennis ball bombs. I'd never seen one before, but I figured it out quickly enough. Fill a hollow ball, rough on the inside, with strike-anywhere match heads. Pitch it away. Let friction take over. Start a fire as far away from you as you could throw it. They probably didn't work all the time, but when they did, I could see how they would be useful. Launched into a pool of gasoline, for instance. Little fires can become big fires.

My dog had been trying to bite down on a bomb.

Suddenly I liked the bandits even less.

Vet was still sitting in front of me, wanting his ball back. He tilted his head.

I sighed, and emptied all the match heads out on the side of the road. Vet sniffed them and sneezed again. I pushed him away with my foot. He backed up and stared at the ball. I spent a few minutes making absolutely sure that every bit of sulfur was gone before throwing the ball down the road. Vet chased after it, and slow though I was, I chased after him. The sun started to set.

After a short distance, I stopped to fashion myself another crutch out of a tree branch. My foot was better, but it was still in no shape to hike across Canada. I'm not sure there is such a thing as 'good enough shape' to hike across Canada. Caribou-shaped, possibly, but humans are really not designed for slowly grazing their way across the tundra.

The landscape as I moved across the world became less hellish and more stable. I felt like I moved through an entirely new planet each hour. I started to realize how cold it was. My skin had been toughening up the entire journey, starting as soon as I left my apartment, but now I was starting to feel a slowing of my body and an ache in my foot. My grandmother used to call it "winter bones." I trudged on anyway, but that night Vet and I cuddled up under the tarp for warmth.

A lot of days went by without much to distinguish one from another. Vet caught a bird. I got lazy and scuffed my foot on the ground, then had to rest for an hour while I cradled it and tried to tell it that everything was going to be okay. When I realized that I was talking to my own foot, I got up and started hobbling again. Sometimes I would see a house and detour hugely, fearing that there would be more and that every former town was a bandit nest. The fear was not so much like the usual metaphorical knife as like a layer of gauze between myself and the world: Some lines of sight and thinking would not come clear, and so rather than risk the things on the other side, I just went around.

If I had thought about it, I might have realized that the world was probably rebuilding around me. I eventually learned that not every still-living person had evacuated, or even needed to. There were still safe places on the world. All over, people were gathering, stocking up supplies, making repairs, getting the power back on, and trying to predict how much more shifting the Earth might do. They knew better than I did that the worst was yet to come. They were even forming good, sensible plans. Governments fell, but the people were moving on. Town halls were being put back into use. There came a time when I should have wondered where all the farmers went, maybe even realized that people were gathering at the nearest hub of civilization to try and regroup, but by the time that may have become apparent to me, I had other worries. So the people went into the towns, and I went into the woods.

My sense of direction was not well-honed in those days. I knew that the sun rose in the east and set in the west. I also knew that the sun never sets on the British Empire, The Sun Also Rises, and Elton John didn't want anyone to let the sun go down on him. I was not totally clear on the fact that the farther north you go, the less the 'American' rules about the sun apply. It does not rise due east. It is not directly overhead at noon. And the nights can get really, really long.

These changes happened in such small increments that I thought I was just going crazy, convincing myself that each night refused to end and each day I was forgetting things and losing time. Finally I noticed that I was getting hungry before it was light out. I still had enough food to eat two meals a day. While I munched during my walking hours, I didn't want another meal until after dark. My stomach knew what time it was. The sun was wrong. After a few more days, though, I didn't have to worry about it, because the sun stopped appearing at all.

I should have expected it. With the world covered in newly active volcanoes and continents shimmying around, the sky was bound to be full of stuff and that stuff was going to come back down. While I was limping my way across the wilderness, that started to happen. Rain. Snow. Hail with little bits of rock or sand in it. I wondered where the sand had been picked up. Maybe it had come all the way from a coastal hurricane. Maybe little pieces of Miami Beach were falling on me. I didn't know much about weather. Regardless of what the whole mess was comprised of, the result was the same: I didn't see the actual sun for days. I spent a great deal of my time hiding under trees or cowering behind rock faces out of the wind. Periods of time stopped blurring together and instead became simplistically defined increments of travel and hiding: Tree, road, rock, rock, road.

Once I saw a moose ambling across the highway. His dark, bulky shape and strong, steady pace now inspired in me a kind of awe. Here was an animal evolved to live in the real world. Humans once had zoos, feeling superior because we had created the iPhone and all animals could do was breed without the aid of doctors, kill other living things with their bare bodies, and survive in all the harshest environments on the planet. Humans have spent a long time being really, really stupid.

I crawled under a tree and flailed around trying to do my basic survival things: Eat, heal, and sleep. The moose moved on, turning south.

CHAPTER TEN
BEING THE NEW HUMAN

Gutting a rabbit, despite having a manual, was not exactly like assembling Ikea furniture. For one thing, the parts are not labeled.

My food was running very low. Vet seemed to get the hint when I started cutting down our meals, and now caught his own disturbingly crunchy rodent dinners most of the time, but I was going to have to stretch what I had a hell of a lot thinner if I wanted to avoid starvation. In this pursuit, I had huddled under yet another tree and studied hunting and trapping, trying to keep my mind in the book and the snow off my eyelashes. I learned to build snares, deadfall traps, and kill pits. Then I started experimenting. What I would actually do with an animal once I caught it, I tried not to think, but finally a stupid rabbit stuck its head under my deadfall trap and I had to figure out how to eat it.

Taking the head off made dealing with it much easier. For one thing, the rabbit's semi-squished face wasn't looking at me while I dissected it. For another, grosser thing, Vet wanted to play with the head, and doing so kept him from sticking his nose in my section of the rabbit.

The inside of the rabbit was a warm mess. There is no

logic to biology. I took what seemed like a sick comfort from the heat, but was also preoccupied with suppressing the Don't-Know-What-I'm-Doing dance my brain cells were trying to execute. Why couldn't rabbits be made of meat all the way through? What the hell was this small purplish thing? How do I get all this stuff out, and was I supposed to do something with it when I did? Rabbits should be more like Ikea furniture. I was good at Ikea furniture.

With the help of the book, I did manage to properly gut the rabbit. The meat was more like a bird than a mammal, but was good. I shared it with Vet.

I also tried to dry out the skin over my little fire so I could use the fur to keep warm, but I got it too close and it burst into flames instead. At least it helped me keep warm for a little while. In about a minute it was reduced to a flap of charcoal and a bad burning-hair smell.

I got better at this process as time and miles went on, and stopping to deal with food was a break from hobbling on my itchy, achy foot. I developed my various methods of turning animals into lunch. Sometimes Vet would run out and bring me back a squirrel, conveniently pre-dead but somewhat slobbered on. When we were passing through farmland, getting wind-whipped and kicking plant stubble, he would bring back mice. My food stash rattled a little in the bottom of my bag, but there was still enough canned tuna and bagged crackers that I just gave the mice back.

Once, Vet brought me one by the tail. It was still alive. I turned around and tried to release it, because I was having a 'civilized person' kind of day, and Vet immediately flopped down on the mouse and rolled it to death. After that, I didn't try to save any more edible skittering critters. It just wasn't that kind of world anymore.

I never did get used to the feel of a dead animal in my hands, or the delicate process of skinning one, but it was like finding that the last thing in the kitchen has been there so long that it's gone to the dark side . . . it might be stale, or squishy, and eating it was not fun, but the more present the hunger is, the less it matters. So the experience was unpleasant. So what. Nothing compares to a full belly and fueled muscles.

Two weeks into Canada, I'd improved at this practice and made myself a big cape of various wildlife. It had a fringe of little rodent skins and a stripe down the spine made of something Vet decapitated that I thought might have been related to a ferret. I tied them all together with fishing line. It was the stupidest-looking thing I had ever worn, but damn, it was warm. At night, I used it as a blanket.

'Shelter' and 'home' used to be pretty synonymous for me. Shelter was a place to put all your stuff and cost seven hundred dollars a month. Now shelter was free anywhere that you could combine a tree, a knife, and a couple hours of effort, but it was never home. Sometimes the impulse would rise to *make* it home: A striking view from an improvised branch-tent or a dread of some upcoming miles of open farmland would make me want to unpack, hang a little picture drawn in berry juice, and start referring to my collection of branches and bows as a studio apartment.

Particularly intense rain or hail would convince me to nap for an additional half a day. Once I started getting farther north, snow did the same. One day early on, I woke up in time to watch a small tornado whip across the fields in front of me. That was a day that I really wanted to stay in my little shelter forever, because the illusion of safety is better than nothing at all, but it wasn't as though I could board up the windows. Vet and I watched the spiraling debris until the tornado hit a far-off tree line and poofed out of existence. Wisps of wind trailed off over the pines and corn stalks fell to earth. I packed up and walked in the nice empty path the tornado had made.

When we got stuck in a long stretch of fields, I would lay down in the dark and cover myself with the fur cape, just an insignificant little bump in the night.

One piece of information that probably saved my life was the following: Do not eat snow. If you can find clean snow, melt it first, then drink it. If a person tries to use their body to heat snow in order to rehydrate, the snow will win.

I still had lighters, matches, and could usually scrounge up something to burn, so I would boil the rain and melt the snow to make sure I was set for water. It wasn't always clean, since a lot of what fell from the sky seemed to be ash and, for whatever reason, sand, so I would boil it, filter it through cloth several times, and then bottle it up. It probably still wasn't good for me, but it was a lot better than dying of dehydration in the Canadian wilderness.

My P.S. predictions of what my life would be like in five years were pretty much screwed. I thought I might be saving up for a deposit on a house. Instead, I was getting splinters trying to build one. Maybe it wasn't so different from working a dead-end job. Either way, I would be suffering a little each day in the hopes of maintaining food and shelter. Still, I could see some clear delineations between my plans and my life now. Walking into a bank and applying for a mortgage probably would not have involved wearing a giant cape made of skinned wildlife. It just wouldn't go with the high heels.

Ever since leaving Portland, I had been carrying my cell phone with me. There was no service, and I hadn't even turned it on because I was saving the battery. What I was saving the battery for, I don't know.

One morning, I shifted my gear and pulled the phone out of a side pocket. Small, black, rounded, featureless . . . it looked like a piece of alien technology in my hand. I didn't even try turning it on. I got up, stretched out my sore, frozen muscles, and threw it into a lake. Vet tried to go after it, even braving a thin sheet of ice near the shore, but it was no use. The thing was gone forever.

Later that day, I scratched my name into a rock and put it in the pocket where the phone had been, having some idea that if anyone found me frozen to death (or inside a bear, or killed by a falling tree, or whatever other equal opportunity death sentence I found out here), they should be able to identify me. The reasoning behind it was stupid. I think there was another, more subtle cause. I got rid of something old, so I replaced it with something new. The combination of evolutionarily greedy nature and capitalist nurture had screwed me up good and proper when it came to material possessions and sheer idiotic behavior. The result was to throw out one useless thing and pick up another to keep from pining over it. The junk is dead; long live the junk.

Vet was no more immune to novelty than I was. Sometimes I threw the ball and got back a rock or a rodent.

Decamping in the morning was hard. The cold had somehow turned my hands into wings, my fingers brushing over things like feathers, unable to bend or feel. When I opened some of the last of my canned meals, I cupped them protectively with my whole body to keep from dropping them.

No one ever includes 'tissues' on the list of emergency supplies. Once the cold started turning from bad to cursed, my sinuses were trying to both freeze and run at all times. I had all kinds of gear with me, but I couldn't blow my nose on a flashlight or a can of tuna. I used a spare shirt for a little while. It froze solid. In the end, I just settled for existing in a state of gross and sniffled a lot. Mucus was not exactly the worst of my problems. The worst of my problems was the sky.

I think, for the purposes of description, I am going to refer to the sky as the 'Blanket of Suck.' The Blanket of Suck was sort of like *distilled* sky: An entire year on the planet's worth of rain, snow, hail, wind, light, dark, and debris came down from it in waves in a single day. Few things are harder to escape than the sky. Except maybe wolves.

When I first noticed them, I learned an awesome truth about nature: Wolves are just not that into you. Vet and I had wandered into the territory of a pack of smallish grey wolves, and they started following us, but I don't know how long they were there before I noticed them because they made no aggressive moves. I just woke up one morning and rolled over in my furry comforter to see Vet standing straight at attention and staring off into the distance. Scrubbing off my glasses and putting them on my face, I could see a grey-brown shape in the distance pouncing into the snow face-first, probably trying to catch mice the same way Vet did. As soon as I stood up, the wolf looked at me and trotted off to the tree line. I watched and waited. At least three more shapes were moving in the woods. I did something I hadn't bothered with for weeks and tied Vet to me with a rope leash. He didn't like it, but I didn't like the idea of him running off to get in a fight with a wolf pack, and since I had the opposable thumbs in our relationship, I won. We took the long way around the tree line.

The wolves followed us for the next three days. I could see at least one of them at any time, if I cared to look. They howled early and often. One night, when I was trying to sleep, they set up a great chorus quite close to my camp.

I thrashed out of my fur blanket and jumped up, shoeless, to yell at my noisy neighbors. Unsure of how to yell, "I've had it with you! It's past midnight! Shut the fuck up!" in the wolf's native language, I howled back at them. My first howl imitation sounded like I had hit my thumb with a hammer. "Owww! Oooowwww!"

With practice came a more Canid noise. "AaooowWWwooo!"

Vet pitched in with a warble.

I kept at it for a long time, until it turned from a silly venting of frustration into a true song. I was loud. I sang about my cold feet in the snow and my last can of soup and all the perceptible miles on every side of me. When I stopped, a wolf came to the top of the ridge nearby and looked at me. Was he wondering what kind of creature I was? If he was, I didn't know what to tell him. I was just being the New Human. Nobody knows what manner of creature that is. Not yet.

Sometimes one of the wolves, a small and mostly cream-colored animal, would run around us. He came within ten yards. He would stare at us the whole time, tongue hanging out, giving off the general impression of creepy stalker dude who drives by your house to show off his car. Eventually, I realized that this was some kind of wolf game. He was having fun. Whether the fun was in scaring me or himself, I don't know, but the bastard was smiling. Once, when he ran back to the safety of dense trees, I could see another wolf run up to him and dance around. I scrubbed my glasses again and watched their interaction. Once I had them in focus, I could practically hear the second wolf talking. "*OMG! You ran right by them! What was it like? Was it awesome? DUDE!*"

That afternoon, I trapped enough small game that I left the wolves some meat on a rock. The next day, we passed out of their territory.

Walking became my new nine to five job. My foot healed slowly and wrong: I could feel the bones crunching sometimes even after the worst of the pain stopped. Still, they ate the miles like tiny insects devouring a dead snake. The snake wasn't entirely dead, of course. The ground would still heave and shake, and the sky snapped back and forth across all points of potential weather. Somewhere out there, a storm god was having a seizure. Down on ground level, I felt like I might do the same, or possibly just implode from discomfort, but I kept on plodding instead.

Humans did a great thing when they invented pavement. Brick, cement, and rubberized asphalt are all surfaces a girl can count on. The wilderness is more fickle. Solid paths get rained on and turn into rivers. Moss may as well grow on stable stones in the shape of a troll face, dumping a person into the half-frozen stream like that was its sole reason for being (I was tempted to try giving it a second mission in life as a food source, but even then, scraping green shit off a rock and eating it proved beyond my drive for sustenance or revenge).

For the curious: Vet is a big dog, but it turns out that he can not be ridden like a pony.

I never once stopped to wonder if I was lost. I was aiming for a huge chunk of the North American continent. If I missed a mark like that, I probably didn't deserve to live anyway. The sun still rose a little sometimes. I only traveled during what passed for the day. The wind was bad at times, but I tucked my chin into my chest and let my legs do their thing.

My pace changed in cycles. Sometimes I ran, and others, I barely walked. It was like a dance lesson I took once . . . slow, slow, fast-tan-go. The dance went on for miles. Once or twice, I slowed until I just leaned against a tree and stopped, but Vet would always come up behind me and head-butt me in the back of the knees to get me going again. I gave him food each time. Encouraging behaviors that increased our survival odds had become a habit.

Sometimes I ran because it was needful. Vet annoyed a bear, and we had to flee from it through the sparse woods. When we reached a field, the bear gave up on us and settled for a warning growl that sounded like twisting metal.

Sometimes I ran because it was joyful, to break my pace and sing silly songs out loud and make heat. Those were the better times, but there was an element of this even in the flights from potential danger: Run, yell, live. Use the heels and toes as living drums and stretch the legs against gravity until they become thin and shaped to the bones, lined with muscles strong but narrow.

Changing weather required changing paces. Frozen days were the best days to run. A warm wind or appearance of sun sometimes melted the snow and dampened the woods, or turned a field into a mud pit, and those were days for slogging and the careful selection of places to put my foot down. When a storm blew in and the wind was bad enough to take down trees, I kept moving from one hiding place to another and held my cloak over my face to keep my breath. Vet had a more one-pace-fits-all approach. His only response to killer weather was to get a few inches lower to the ground. Sometimes nice days were the hardest ones to get started on. I didn't want to walk. I just wanted to choose a rock and soak up the little sun that was available. On the rare occasion that I did give myself a few hours off, the lack of forward motion started to get to me, like being on solid ground after a long time at sea. Something in me was always rocking. Instead of taking breaks, I usually just took a beautiful day slowly instead. Loud noises gave me only momentary pause. One morning, I looked around to find the source of a sound that turned out to be a small avalanche. I was a safe distance away. I slowed down to watch it. The sound lasted longer than the avalanche. For full minutes after the snow stopped roiling, I could still hear the creak of it settling. Nature was flexing the hinges on the skylight of the world. Vet and I stopped to listen and eat, then ambled on.

I came to a highway and bolted across it like a deer, fleeing for the woods on the other side.

I was holding up against the world. I built a lot of fires to stay warm. I kept two water bottles and rotated them, so that one was always drinkable and one was always melting snow. Backpack space was now abundant, so I collected firewood and bark throughout the day. I continued to swerve around any sign of people without even thinking. Vet was catching all of his own food. He seemed to be doing fine out here in the wild, even if he was a just a big short-haired member of a domestic species. I imitated him in many ways, including sleeping habits, and I started to wonder if pouncing on small birds with my teeth was the next logical thing to do. Finally, after weeks of trekking through the woods, it occurred to me that I still had a handgun and little ammo left in my bag.

Since I still had a gun, I made several attempts to take down a large animal, but for the longest time I couldn't find any. The Big Game Hunter II arcade machine in my old bar had been very misleading. I did encounter a moose or two while walking, but wasn't prepared. Also, I was worried about what might happen if I only wounded a moose. Those bastards are huge. The gun was small.

I was spending more time hungry, but still I would alternate between salivating over the wildlife and wanting to take it home and cuddle it. I've got a scattershot heart.

After a week of trying, I finally brought my gun to bear in time to take down a white-tailed deer. My experience with the deer was much like the first rabbit, but larger. It turned out to be food for a week and a skin large enough that I made a one-piece hood for my patchwork fur cape. The fire from that night burned for many hours, drying the skin, cooking the venison, and bringing my core temperature so high that I could almost believe I was back in civilization. Watching bark and branches burn was better than television in every way. By the end, the fire was hot enough to dry out some green wood for burning the next day.

There is a feeling of peace that I had once achieved by crossing off everything on my to-do list, having all my bills paid, and sitting down with a large pizza and a book.

This same feeling can be achieved with a dead deer, a tree, and a lighter.

The thumb of my glove also caught fire. Fortunately, everything outside my campfire's sphere of influence was still wet and snowy, so I just punched a slush pile to put it out.

For the next two months, I followed the same pattern. Wake up. Feed myself. Walk miles. Figure out how to feed myself some more. Build a fire. Prop up some pine boughs. Pet the dog. Don't die.

CHAPTER ELEVEN
P.S. I LOVE YOU

There were a lot of empty miles, so I filled them with memories.

Mostly I fantasized about P.S. things. It was months that I had spent living this way, but some buried past-life brain cells still knew that certain things had been real and good and wanted them back. I wanted a cheeseburger from Alberta Street Pub and I wanted to drive to Lloyd Center to buy myself a new fuzzy bathrobe. I wanted to shop for socks and spend completely unnecessary amounts of time debating between twenty pair that were exactly the same save for color or pattern. I wanted to kick off my boots, scrub myself down, and put on some silly high heels, even though the concept now seemed totally alien. I wanted to get a paycheck and blow it at the bar. More than anything, I wanted to waste an entire day of my life on the couch, staring at my computer, learning about whale sharks on Wikipedia and talking to strangers in Japan, totally blasé about my own technology-given godlike powers. This now-unfathomable activity would be accompanied by ice cream. Occasionally, it might be interrupted by texting. I would not speak to another human being in person all day. Kind of like now, I guess. The craving for internet lounging was so strong that I wanted to log into my Neopets account from seventh grade and tell my little pixel creatures that everything would be all right. A layer of caked snow crept up the legs of my pants as I slogged on.

I composed a list in my head.

P.S. I Love You
(Things I Miss About Civilization)

Electricity
Hot water
Roofs
Neighborhood bars
Boredom
Skype
Yoga classes
Frisbee with strangers in public parks
Weekends
Holidays
Knowing what day it is
Being able to update my status on Facebook
Fast food
YouTube videos of cats destroying rolls of toilet paper
Gas stations and grocery stores
Cell phones
Being surrounded by more people than you can count
Radio stations
Caffeinated everything

Snow plows
Cashews
Photos NASA took from outer space
Meat so processed it looks like it was never an animal

Once upon a time, all of these things were mine.

But the real me, the me that spends time in quiet contemplation in the little tea house of my soul, knows that I don't live there anymore. I belong here.

I belong with the sky and the distance now.

While I was trudging along, thinking these thoughts, I got my foot stuck in a dead raccoon. That's life, I guess.

CHAPTER TWELVE
SASKATCHEWAN

By the time Ives found me, my transformation into Wilderness Survival Mab was long since complete. Vet and I lived as a single unit, working like we shared thoughts when all we shared was proximity. All aspects of my physical appearance had gone feral. There was rabbit blood in my short, ragged hair to keep it plastered back on my head and out of my face. Spoken language was a thing of the past, a concept that belonged only in memories.

I was climbing a forested hill when Vet detected Ives. The dog stopped short, and I looked down at him immediately. If he was upset, it might mean a bear or a bad guy. Instead, Vet gave one jerky half-wag of his tail, then another a few seconds later. Soon his tail was thumping back and forth like someone had wound up a giant rubber band inside him. This was not one of the signals I was used to, and I didn't know what Vet was telling me until Ives came over the hill, saw us, and put up his hands.

Tail wagging, of course, means *friend.*

I did not react as well as I might have. Ives, despite his completely inoffensive gesture, was a very tall man with a rifle strapped to his back and a straggly wild look much like my own, so of course I assumed he was going to try to kill me, even if he was just standing there with his hands up. My gun was buried in my bag, unloaded, so I tried shooting my mouth off instead. The voice that came out was creaky. It sounded only a little like sensible words to me, but it was close enough to communication.

"Hi-my-name-is-Mab-I'm-lost-and-I've-come-a-very-long-way-and-this-is-Vet, and we're walking together and did you know that people are less likely to shoot you if you're talking to them I read that once but I think I'm just supposed to keep talking instead of telling you that but look . . . uh . . . I've made it across most of a continent and I would really like it if I didn't do all that just to get shot now so if you kill me it's really going to ruin my day-"

He laughed a little and spread his arms wider apart, like he was going to take flight from the top of the hill. Vet ran up and sniffed him all over, then laid down and rolled onto the stranger's feet and knocked him over. This dispelled the fear. I slogged the rest of the way up the slushy hill and stood over man and dog as they lay on the ground.

"Hi . . . you're the first human being I've spoken to in three months. Can I try that again?"

He reached up his hand.

"I'm Ives. You're safe."

"I'm Mab. I was pretty safe already, but *fuck* is it good to see you."

"Great. Good. Yeah. I don't want to make any sudden movements and freak you and the dog out or anything, but I'm going to get up now."

And then . . . then there was a moment. A moment where Crazy Mab, given many chances to come into her own and having been given much credit for ideas that kept me alive, said *kill him. Kill him before he hurts you or Vet. Kill him now.*

Less than a second passed. I gave him a hand up instead.

"Where are you headed?"

I had been operating on simple thoughts for a long time, so I can probably be excused for this, but I blurted out, "Canada."

Ives gave me a slow, assessing look.

"You're in Canada. So . . . congratulations? You made it?"

"Um . . . no, I mean . . . damn, it has been a long time since I've had to use more than three words out loud. I read about the Canadian Shield in a book. It sounded like the safest place to be. So I headed there."

"Hey, awesome. That's why we came here, too."

" . . . Here?"

Ives indicated the Northeast view with a glance and a tilt of his head. Looking out, I saw some barren rock and forest. From this elevation, a few small lakes were also visible.

"Most stable place in North America," he said. "You're standing on it."

I should have shouted and danced and hugged him. Instead, once the fact set in, I gave one decisive nod and started setting up camp. All I wanted to do was sleep forever. Ives watched me work. Once I had a little branch-nest to hunker down in, he sat down outside it and started a fire. Vet stayed between Ives and myself, but hardly seemed protective. He was obviously quite in favor of this new person. I went to sleep. It may have been strange, but it was my gut reaction to having reached my destination. There was really nothing else left to do.

I slept for almost a day. Ives waited for me. When I

woke up, I was baffled and startled at his existence all over again. He and Vet sat around the fire looking at me with nearly identical amicable expressions. When I sat down with them, Vet made the first move by hanging his tongue out and grinning. Ives stuck his tongue out at Vet. Vet licked him. This effectively made Ives one of us.

"So . . . " I said.

"Yeah. It's okay. We've had a couple other people like you, who had a rough trip. It can mess you up for a little while. But I promise, I just want to help you out here. Where did you come from?"

"Portland. Oregon."

"Holy shit."

"Yeah."

"That's the farthest I've heard of. I thought that whole part of the continent was just, like . . . um."

"Yeah."

"Well, you're here now, right? Let's get back to NightsReach and set you up."

I stared at him.

"NightsReach?"

"I can't believe there are still . . . people." I said.

"Sure, yeah. Well, James brought a lot of them with him – this was pretty much all his plan. Plus, Killer had her own gang. They were going all the way to Alaska, but they heard about NightsReach in one of the towns so they stopped here instead. People are actually talking about us a lot. It's pretty awesome. NightsReach has gotten a lot bigger than we ever expected."

People? I thought. *Towns?*

First, I froze up. Trying to shift realities ground the large, rudimentary gears of thought that I'd been running on to a halt. *People. Towns.*

Then I did a pretty passable impression of that mall mannequin so many miles ago, and lost my head.

"Everyone died. How the fuck can there still be towns?! Everyone got buried and burned and evacuated and dropped into the middle of the planet because there was no place safe to go! There can't be towns! I was in Portland and it was just me! Me, and a few *dead* people! And Vet! *Who the hell are you talking about?!*"

"There were-" Ives started, but I couldn't stop.

"No! No. No. I don't know who the hell you are but they're all dead. Gone. Everyone is gone. I've got rabbit blood in my hair and there is no one left to give a shit because everyone is gone!" I started crying. Crying was bad, not only embarrassing but a waste of water and a good way to freeze the skin off my face. I had to stop and I didn't know how. So I started screaming instead.

One long, loud, incoherent scream, straight up into the sky.

I would do this more than once in the coming months, but never again with someone else around to witness it, because when I brought my head back down I could see that Ives was suffering, too. I was venting all the built-up fear and poison and because he was there, he was getting hit with it. I stopped everything.

"It's okay," he said. "You'll be okay. I know how it is. Well, I don't, I guess, but we had one guy who wandered into the Reach, looked around, and then smiled and shot himself in the head. Pretty sure the way it works is, if you can scream it out, or run it out or cry it out or whatever you need to do, you're going to make it." He tried to smile. "Let's just get you to NightsReach."

For the last few miles, Ives and I held hands. He just reached out for me and I accepted. I'm not sure why, but it made all the difference in the world. What might have been screaming sobs became just a silent face leak. Walking became a means of transportation instead of a way of life. He held me and he freed me. Humans can do that for each other.

While we walked, we compared notes about the Great Suck. (Ives called it the Great Fuck-All, and since I called it the Suck, we compromised.)

A lot of our information matched up. I told him in detail about my experiences with exploding mountains, the entire Cascade Chain going up like fireworks.

I learned later that a group of former mountains farther south in that range were called the Three Sisters. Early settlers had named them Faith, Hope, and Charity. That information reopened a great, sucking wound in my heart from those early times . . . Faith, Hope, and Charity, gone up in ash and flames.

NightsReach was like a village wrapped in a circus wrapped in an elementary school play about farming. It's not much of a description, but I didn't have much of a coherent impression. Everything blurred together.

There were people all over the place. Most of them were younger, spanning the teen years and dropping off in population density after the age of forty. Some looked like preppie snowboarders, but at least half of them looked like they got lost on their way to Burning Man. Three girls wearing neon faux-fur hats with bear ears on them walked by. A man and a woman wearing Doc Martins, snow pants, and tank tops were working on the last tree house in a line of five. A couple of guys in their early twenties were throwing snowballs away from the camp as hard as they could, and another guy with dreadlocks and a coyote skin around his neck was firing a high-tech hunting bow to bust the snowballs up with practice arrows. It almost looked like . . . fun.

Then someone in one of the tree houses started crying and screaming. Two faces, full of concern, turned towards the sound and scrambled up the ladder. Mankind might be regrouping, but things were still not okay. I watched the dreadlock-man shoot at snowballs and tried to forget for a minute. Ives slowed down to wait for me, but when it looked like I might retreat into overwhelmed catatonia, he grabbed my hand again and led me towards the biggest fire.

A little ways into the camp, we passed a wooden signpost. I pulled on Ives's arm. "That sign." I said.

"Yeah?"

"That sign doesn't say NightsReach. That sign, unless I have totally lost the ability to read, says NightsRetch."

"Not everyone here is big on spelling. Or English. I guess it works either way."

"So this place is actually called NightsReach?"

"Yes."

"Why?"

"It's sort of a pun. We're right near Kingsmere Lake. Kings, knights . . . I don't know, really. Ask James, he's the one who decided we needed a name and that was it. Personally, I probably would have planted a big candy-striped pole in the middle and called us the Island of Misfit Toys."

I laughed harder than I should have.

"Or maybe FreezingMan," I suggested.

Ives snickered and continued to explain.

"We're still kind of a mess," he said. "I guess that's pretty much to be expected, but there are towns getting their shit together a lot faster than us. Cities, even. I hear Calgary is doing great, but we only know because some people defected from civilization anyway. They think this is their chance to go live off the land and be real men. Most of them are great guys. There was only one we had to chase out. He thought being a Man in the Wilderness here with us meant being a Neanderthal and being handed large chunks of meat and virgins . . . totally toxic. We sent him further north. He's either been eaten by a bear by now or he's found his people among the Alaska refugees.

"Anyway, we're a little slow, getting it together. It doesn't help that there is no . . . What do you call it. Trade language. Common tongue."

"Lingua franca," I said.

"Thank god, you'll add to our overall village brain power. I love 'em all but we've got enough village idiots. Anyway. People here speak mostly English or French, but only a couple people speak both, and somewhere on the trip here Killer picked up this Bosnian kid that no one understands. He's picking up both English and French, though, a hell of a lot faster than we were learning to understand him, so I'm thinking he might be the one to save our asses communication-wise in a month or so. Frigging kid speaks more French than I do already, and he started picking up English first."

"You," I said, "Are you American?"

Ives laughed.

"Not for a couple years now. I moved up here to . . . you know, I'm not even sure what, now. Be Canadian and get free health care and wash dishes and learn to fish. Or something. But I guess I'm always going to be mostly American. Can you tell? Do I sound like New York to you?"

New York City is washed out way past the GW bridge, totally fucked, squashed and tilted and buried in itself and popped like a balloon full of brick confetti. Last I knew, New York was unrecognizable all the way to Tappan Zee, and the Palisades Parkway was covered in rust and death. Suddenly, these facts did not matter one bit, because he did. He sounded like New York to me.

"Bronx," I guessed.

"Hah. Damn. You from the city?"

"Once upon a time."

"So . . . what are New Yorkers supposed to do to celebrate when they meet? Honk and flip each other off?"

"I think, in the event of natural disaster, we are allowed to hug. But just the once."

We did.

Then Ives introduced me to his plucky band of survivalists, who I am sure would have saved me from zombies if the chance had arisen. Instead, they saved my brain from itself.

There were five people around the bonfire. Each one introduced themselves, but my skills at picking up new names and faces were a little rusty, so for a while I thought of them as Pink Hair, The Sweatshirt, Generic College Student, WarriorGirl, and WarriorGuy. They were the crew Ives had started out with from Regina. Regina hadn't fared as well as Calgary on the social reconstruction front, and when gunshots became normal background noise, Ives and the girl I was calling Pink Hair grabbed the others and packed up his truck. Their road trip ended in NightsReach.

Ives was blinking rapidly as he told his story. At first I thought he was reacting to the smoke, but his voice started cracking while he was summarizing their situation. His descriptions of Regina and their trip came in shorter and shorter sentences. Finally, he just said, "It was bad."

"There was one last crazy thing," Pink Hair told us while she stirred the fire. "I was holding my own, staying in my house, thinking I could make it through. I boarded up the windows. There were a lot of strangers around, people coming up from the States and in from the woods. I stopped lighting candles or using anything that would give me away. It was bad enough that the basic civil services broke down, and no one came to collect the trash, but in the last week or so we were there . . . no one came to collect the bodies. There was a man in a suit with a big bloody bullet hole in it, and he died sitting up on a bus stop bench across the street from my house. A truck went by, and someone hung out the window and knocked his head off with a baseball bat . . . like a mailbox. I've been having nightmares where I end up like the man on the bench ever since. After I saw that, I started packing my bags. I don't even remember doing it. I just remember Ives picking me up on the way out of town."

Ives started in with some comforting banter. I couldn't follow the conversation very well, especially with the occasional interjected French, but they didn't seem to expect much from me. Newcomers were assumed to be in a state of shock until they proved otherwise.

WarriorGirl left for a minute and came back with a canvas grocery bag, which she dropped in front of me. I opened it. The bag was full of food, chemical heat packs, and clean socks. At the bottom, I found two bottles of beer.

"We've been rationing pretty well," WarriorGirl said, "But this is your new-girl Welcome to NightsReach basket. Also, we're going to cook a few hundred hot dogs tonight before they go bad, so that should be a nice first meal of the rest of your life." She stuck her tiny, ringed hand in my bloody hair, roughed it up, and smiled at me.

I wasn't any good at it just then, but I joined the conversation anyway. We talked for a long time about nothing much, scrunching ourselves back down into the comfy bed of normalcy a little bit at a time. I drank the beer. When it was empty, I stopped and goggled at it in my hand for a minute, thinking, what do I do with this? Put it in the recycling bin?

The Sweatshirt tapped me on the shoulder.

"You throw it in the fire," he said. "We all did it, and it's kind of become a thing. You smash one in the fire and it's like . . . like letting go of whatever happened to you. You know. Before this. You break one and be done with it."

That sounded like an excellent idea to me.

I stood, and used every strand of my new feral muscle to cast the bottle into the flames. It cracked like lightning. The fire danced away from it, then closed over the shards.

Thus ended the reign of Queen Mab of the Broken Glass.

The first night, there were hot dogs for massive, barbeque-style dinner, and I got to bathe in a fire-heated tin tub. I'm pretty sure the bath was a horse trough, and it was lukewarm at best, but it was still a miraculous evening at the spa to me and I stayed in the steaming water for more than an hour. When I got out, the water was so disgusting I dumped it out and put fresh snow in the tin to melt. There were towels hanging on sawhorses around the fire, and I wrapped myself in two giant beach towels and sat on a sawhorse to dry off in the heat. My foot was still mangled, but I tried not to look at it. I really couldn't be bothered. That night, I slept right there under the sawhorse with a towel draped over me. Other people walked around feeding the fires. I had nothing productive to do.

The next day, Ives tried to give me a tree house, but

since Vet couldn't get up and into one, I started building my own on the ground. There was real lumber to work with. Hammers and nails got passed around like booze and cigarettes. Anyone able-bodied and free was working on building various shelters: Small, flexible, as proof as possible against water and earthquake. These were occupied at random. I spent hours arranging my few possessions in the new shack. Ives brought by some blankets, and I set up beds for Vet and I, separate but only by a few inches. In the course of a day, I made myself a one-room house and moved right in. While unloading my backpack, my hands found the stone with my name carved on it. I set it outside the door.

For the next three or four days, I slept and read my few remaining books. Someone I didn't know dropped by on Ives's suggestion to bring me more, but they were mostly romance novels. I used them as a pillow and learned more about tracking game instead.

People dropped by and introduced themselves. I met a man with one useless arm, mangled worse than my foot. A woman came by with mostly-still-edible fruit and talked to me for a while, but she wore a scarf over her head, pulled all the way down to her eyebrows. She scratched at it periodically, then finally cursed at the scarf and removed it. She had burns covering most of her head. One ear was healing into a mass that resembled a rumpled horn.

My next visitor seemed completely whole at first. He introduced himself, made with the light-hearted flirtation because 'there's only so many single women around' and 'I seemed like an awesome one,' and we talked about dating sites from the Internet of Yore. I mentioned movies. He said he would miss sci-fi the most. I asked if he was into Firefly. He stumbled through another half of a sentence before starting to cry, excusing himself, and staggering out of my shelter. Vet whined with concern, but I just rubbed the dog behind the ears and thought about how we're all damaged now.

On my last day of self-imposed solitary, James came to see me. He was older than a lot of us, but still only in his thirties. James was a redhead, like me, and in the initial awkward introductions we still managed to fluff our hair and make ginger jokes.

James had founded NightsReach. I expected him to be a doctor, a detective, or maybe distinguished ex-military, and his extended vocabulary and pronunciation didn't dissuade me, but it turned out that P.S. James was a truck driver who delivered bulk food. He was dropping off a semester's worth of powdered eggs and soda syrup to a small college when the world started falling apart and students started fleeing. James was in the right place at the right time, with chains on his tires and a potential destination in mind. He saved a truck full of people. As a kid, he spent time at Kingsmere Lake with his family, and somewhere along the line he'd learned about the geography like I had, so he brought them here.

While James told us his story, Vet cuddled up to his feet and fell asleep. I ate a granola bar.

James had gone to college, too, with the intention of becoming an archeologist. There were fewer openings in his chosen field than he could have hoped for, so he ended up getting his CDL and driving trucks. Still, he had a base knowledge many people lived without, and had been adding to it. So when James came around, he explained to me what had happened, and what was likely to happen next.

What had happened, when it came down to it, was simple. The earth shifted. The things living on it got screwed. Deep sea creatures boiled in their trenches and birds dropped out of the sky. Humans, having populated the most geologically treacherous areas possible, took a big hit despite being the dominant species. That much I knew. Hearing James say it out loud was almost helpful. The ways he summed it up were clean and bloodless.

Now that I think of it, some of that same antiseptic method of revelation may have come into my own account. Though I can't ignore what happened to the world, my telling of it was just as simplified. Maybe no one has the capacity to tell it otherwise. At any rate, James named people, places, and times, and turned the end of the world into a history lesson.

John Green once wrote, "If you don't imagine, nothing ever happens at all." This was probably meant to be encouraging, but now we were all turning it on its head, refusing to imagine. If we refused to think about it, the demolition of cities and the humans buried in the earth and the beautiful birds of prey choking on ash plumes might never have happened at all. There was no father watching his child be swallowed by a volcano in Memphis if I didn't picture him. There were no dead pets or starving survivors. We dehydrated these events by denying them our imaginations, putting the end of the world in dry storage as a history lesson until we were prepared to deal with it again. Names, dates, places. We had no thoughts or feelings left to give them.

This would have simplified my life completely, if dealing with the past was the only thing that needed doing.

It was not.

James smiled at the end of his History of the End of the World, and made some hemming and hawing noises.

"You should know . . . " he said, then left it in the air for a minute while he arranged his face again and again, aiming for neutral and missing each time.

"You should know that it's not over. It may have just started."

This felt correct to me.

"What's next?" I said.

"Well . . . " James blinked too many times. "It's like this. When the planet does something this big, historically speaking, the whole thing has to reset. I don't think this big whirling rock is done for good, but there's going to be more. The volcanoes are already messing up the atmosphere, so the weather is going to change. A lot. We're trying to prepare for an ice age, even though we're hoping for more of a 'forty days and nights of rain' kind of thing. An ice age is more likely. This is probably what's called an extinction-level event . . . the planet is just not a good place for us anymore, and we might end up wiped off the face of the damn thing. Not just us, you and me, or us, people, or even us, mammals, but most of us, from bacteria on up. But it's not a sure thing. We've got technology that no other species has ever had, and when it comes to food, water, and shelter . . . well, we're a pretty resourceful species and this is a camp full of pretty resourceful people. We might get by.

"But we've got to start setting ourselves up now. We're going to be stocking up, rationing, and even working on a more permanent underground shelter, just in case we don't get the simple forty days and nights like we're hoping. Just in case."

Vet grumbled at James's feet. Even in his sleep, Vet knew there was mounting worry in the room, despite James's reassuring 'just in cases.' The worry was soft, but the knowledge was hard: Life was going to be difficult and we might be screwed anyway. Still, I let James be reassuring for a while.

"Well, anyway. I just wanted to give you a debriefing

when I heard that we got you out of the woods. Where did you come from, anyway?"

"Portland. Oregon."

"Holy shit."

"Yeah."

James shook my hand and left my cabin.

That night, there was someone outside my cabin playing a guitar. I didn't have any windows, but I sat in my door to listen.

Since arriving at NightsReach, I felt like I had been doing a lot of nodding and smiling. At least, I hoped it was smiling. The idea that my face actually betrayed all the things I had been feeling was just horrifying. Still, I knew that I had been giving short answers and making wooden movements in my short public forays. I was submerged in society again, but I didn't feel like a complete person.

When the mystery guitar player went from tuning and fussing to playing nineties pop-rock, I sang along. Third Eye Blind and Matchbox Twenty connected two strangers in the dark. More people wandered by and joined in. Someone started a new campfire in front of my cabin. Little pieces of my heart started to fuse back together.

WarriorGuy walked out of the darkness and passed me a wine bottle. I drank and gave it to a stranger. We all sang a song no one could remember the name of. Hours passed this way.

Finally, a storm blew up and people wandered off. These clouds brought rain instead of snow, putting out the fire and chasing me back into my cabin. I was sick of being wet. The guitarist retreated to whatever tree house or fort he called home.

This time I didn't read. I had learned all I could from my books and gone through all the other useful ones in the camp, speed-reading through history and sociology and psych and engineering, so I just laid in my blanket-nest with one hand on Vet and the other across my chest, thinking. Outside, the storm walked around the wild, reaching down fingers of lightning to play the world like a piano. Staccato.

In the next few days, I left my cabin more often. Vet escorted me everywhere I went, but was always friendly to strangers. I took more baths in the tin trough than entirely necessary. I helped sort, store, and prepare food. I heard people's stories. I told them mine, but only in short clips or summaries. I told nearly everyone about the coyote in the grocery store. They loved it.

I learned about the animals around camp, as well. People had been going out and saving livestock from farms big and small, so we had cows, sheep, chickens, and a few other dogs. Vet made some new friends. There was also a small black and white cat. No one knew where it came from, but it showed up one day and didn't seem inclined to leave.

One night, Ives stopped by my new place to introduce me to one last person. It's a good thing they came together, because if I had seen her on my own, I might have shot her.

Killer ducked into my cabin behind Ives. She had a Bettie Page haircut and blue star tattoos. I would have recognized the Bandit Queen by silhouette alone, and now she was five feet in front of me. I reached for my gun. Vet stood up, lowering his head. Killer put up her hands and said "Oh, shit. Hold on."

The three of us spent a wide-eyed minute explaining things to each other. I went first, and loudly. Ives tried to make sense of what was happening. Finally, Killer sat down cross-legged, keeping her hands in the air, and told her story. It started with the words, "I had to." Those words were a hell of a better excuse than they used to be. I moved away from my handgun and listened.

Killer was an actress and a part-time bartender. She saved her own life by swaggering into the Bandit Palace and making herself useful. At first, she thought she had found a new home. Then the Bandit King started killing newcomers. She could either play along until the time was right, or object and get shot. She played along.

Killer pulled off the greatest bluff in poker of all time because when she arrived at the Bandit Palace, she didn't know how to play cards. She picked it up from watching, and fast, because the pressure to participate and be 'one of the guys' was on. She was convincingly drunk and loud and violent. Sometimes she killed the people who came down the Crowsnest Highway herself. Unlike the Bandit King, she tried to make it quick and painless.

Two nights after I ran from them, she ended the Bandit King's life in his sleep and cleared out the rest of the dangerous ones. Whoever was left came with her to NightsReach.

She told her story in a level tone. I thought it was probably true, and wanted to accept what she had done without judging her, but I had one thing I couldn't bury.

"You did all that, and now you call yourself Killer?"

She shrugged.

"Sometimes you've gotta own it."

We all had our stories.

NightsReach had collected many tools, but most were in bad shape. Snow shovels were chipped and covered in duct tape. Spades with broken handles and clippers with dull, notched blades were piled in the back of a makeshift shed. I learned to work on them and spent a few hours sharpening hatchets and oiling them; Motor oil for the blade, linseed for the handle. Ives came by to help and say that he was glad he found me. I ate lunch with dirty hands.

Finally, I had to stop lurching along, no matter how helpful I was being. I sat down with Ives and his crew around the fire that night. Someone had thrown together a stew with fresh meat. No two of us had matching bowls. Mine was ceramic with pastel stripes. It was a patchwork service, but it was a civilized dinner all the same. Before the food was even gone, we ran out of ideas for small talk. Ives kept glancing my way. I might not have noticed, except I couldn't stop looking at him, either, thinking about what he had done for me. I put down my bowl.

"Hey, Ives."

"Yeah."

"Thanks for finding me."

We almost had our sappy moment in time. Then Ives snorted.

"Yeah, well, thanks for being a productive member of society again. You're going to save our asses, Miss Portland, Oregon. Holy shit!"

We all smiled. Only a little.

They were all looking at me. Finally, WarriorGirl said, "So . . . what was your apocalypse like?"

I didn't know what to say. What almost came out of my mouth was, *Fine, how about yours?*, but I stopped it just in time. There was a long silence. The fire popped. No one looked away from me. I sneezed. Not wanting them to think that a sneeze was my entire comment on the end of the world, I said the first thing that came to mind.

"Well . . . I wish it had been zombies."

And they laughed.

Laughter is a rarer thing now. Often, we're too tired, or too unsure. Often it seems like there has been too much death and violence and loss to laugh, and even if none of it happened to us, we felt the Suck that happened to our species, looming as a cloud in our big picture. It was going to be a while before anything was really okay again. Until then, we were a people of eyes with damp waterlines, slightly open mouths, uncertain but gentle manners. Laughing was for good times. Good times might be a long time in coming.

Still, I realized two things. One was that her question should really be answered in some more detailed and enduring way: How was the apocalypse? We always ask after people's weekends, their workdays, even their trips to the dentist. How could we stop asking this question now? Suddenly I was amazed that we hadn't just been spending all our time together walking around asking that simple question. *How was your apocalypse?*

The second thing I came to realize, though not for a week or two, is that laughter is the best of the civilized world, and since my survival of the Suck was the greatest joke I knew, I should tell it.

Tomorrow, I'll be leaving NightsReach on an extended supply run. We need things. I am reasonably well-equipped to find them and bring them back. I have my giant fur cloak, and Vet, and the sum of my experience. Many people in the Reach are in no condition to make the trip, but I am.

Picture Queen Mab astride her new snowmobile, her barbarian cape snapping in the wind and a big black dog at her side, bravely heading back out into the wilderness to help save her little improvised town. Adding some theme music would be nice, too. I imagine that "Mayhem" song from the tape I found, and I'll probably be singing it at the top of my lungs when I fire up that snowmobile, but any suitably epic music is fine. If the weather holds, there might even be a sunset to ride into.

And let me fucking tell you, I am ready.

ABOUT THE AUTHOR

Rachel Sharp is an author and lifetime member of the Somewhat Eccentric Creative Person's Club (which she just made up). She has won multiple silly little writing awards that nobody has ever heard of.

She lives in New York with her partner and her boundless sense of inappropriate humor, and is currently working the second Planetary Tarantella book, A Word and a Bullet.

Made in the USA
San Bernardino, CA
30 January 2016